Born to be wild!

Dylan gunned the engine a couple of times and then swerved into rush-hour traffic. I closed my eyes and felt a scream work its way up my throat. But I was so intent on hanging on to Dylan and bracing myself against the noise and the wind, my voice died out.

This was my first ride on a motorcycle, and the first five minutes were awful. The roar of the engine, the feeling of nothing between me and the road. I clung to Dylan as if he were a life jacket in the storm of late-afternoon commuters. But as soon as we turned onto a small, quiet street I began to enjoy the ride.

"I like this," I tried to tell him. But I don't think Dylan could hear me through his helmet. *This might be my first time on his Harley, but it's definitely not my last.*

I savored being a bad girl as Dylan came to a stop. I threw my head back into the wind and laughed. I wasn't doing anything bad or wrong. I was just having fun, trying new things. Trying to find the real Naomi Peters.

Don't miss any of the books in *Love Stories* —the romantic series from Bantam Books!

How to Kiss a Guy

ELIZABETH BERNARD

BANTAM BOOKS
NEW YORK · TORONTO · LONDON · SYDNEY · AUCKLAND

RL 6, age 12 and up

HOW TO KISS A GUY
A Bantam Book / April 1995

Produced by Daniel Weiss Associates, Inc.
33 West 17th Street
New York, NY 10011

ISBN: 0-553-56662-8

Published simultaneously in the United States and Canada

Bantam Books are published by Bantam Books, a division of Bantam
Doubleday Dell Publishing Group, Inc. Its trademark, consisting of the
words "Bantam Books" and the portrayal of a rooster, is Registered in
U.S. Patent and Trademark Office and in other countries. Marca
Registrada. Bantam Books, 1540 Broadway, New York, New York 10036.

PRINTED IN THE UNITED STATES OF AMERICA

OPM   0 9 8 7 6

To Naomi, who asked me to write another romance, and to Joe Marraffino and Andrea Bendewald, who in different ways shared their craft of acting.

Chapter One

MY NAME IS Naomi Peters, and just by looking at me, you'd never think I was a girl
with a secret. Two secrets, actually.

Not the dark or scary kind of secret. My dad is
not a secret agent, and our family—my little sister
Karen, my mom, our cat Pebbles—is definitely *not*
hiding from some drug cartel in the Boston suburb
where we live. No, nothing like that. I'm really just
an ordinary fifteen-year-old. But there are some
things about me most people would never guess.

For instance, even though I'm a sophomore at
Paul Revere High, I still devour romance novels
like gummi bears.

Most of my friends like romance novels. But
when they get a romance of their own, they usually
stop reading. Not me. Even though I've been dating
Josh for months, I'm still hooked on love stories.

1

You know the kind—where one kiss sends your whole life spiraling into orbit. Like when the hero *knows* the heroine is his destiny—and he'll go to the ends of the earth to win her love. *That's* what I call romantic. In real life, with Josh, I keep waiting for the romance part to kick in.

Maybe Josh Davidson is not the stuff great love stories are made of.

Maybe I'm not either. But on the cold November day when the cast list was posted for our school production of *Beauty and the Beast,* I began to wonder.

I was so excited. I wore all new clothes to school that day, including the cowboy boots I'd saved all summer to buy, and the long denim skirt that made my no-color eyes look a definite blue. Though it was a gray, rainy morning and most kids were feeling glum as glue about midterms and the Revere High football squad's third loss in a row, I felt great as I hurried toward the school auditorium. Almost lucky . . . as if something really special was going to happen.

My whole life was about to change. I was sure of it. I—shy, sweet Naomi, whom everyone liked but wrote off as a "brain" on the fast track to Harvard prelaw—had gone and done something outrageous! Without checking it out with my parents first, or having two hundred endless discussions with my best friend Amanda, or even thinking of mentioning my plan to Josh, I had skipped honors study session at the school library and tried out for the school play—for the *lead* in the school play.

This was something people would *never* have guessed about me. Everyone—my parents, my best friends—had already decided I would be a lawyer, but I've always—secretly—wanted to be an actress. And *Beauty and the Beast* could give me my start.

"Pipe down, people!" The voice belonged to Dave Martin, president of Masques, the Revere High drama club. He stood in front of the bulletin board outside the auditorium. Lockers were thrown open and banged shut. Everyone seemed late for class. And all of us who had tried out for the play jockeyed to be the first to see the cast list. The noise level was extraordinary, even for our large, over-crowded school.

"Hey, guys, back off so I can post this list."

The crowd obeyed. They gave big, burly Dave another two inches in which to wield his pushpins.

"Where did all these people come from?" gasped my best friend, Amanda Zukowski. When I'd told Amanda last night about tryouts, she thought I was nuts, but admitted that I was pretty brave to get up in front of all those people and audition. She also thought I didn't stand a chance of being cast. Sophomores don't get leads, she'd reminded me. Especially inexperienced sophomores who are probably taller than any guy in the drama club. Still, she and Max Munoz and Josh had detoured en route to homeroom today just to give me some moral support.

I needed it. I don't know exactly what possessed me to try out, except that next to heavy-duty romance, I crave stardom more than anything. That's my biggest secret of all. Since I was five and played the tallest angel with the biggest halo at the Sunday school Christmas pageant, I've lusted for Hollywood, or Broadway, or TV. I've just been too shy to try.

My first and only stage experience had been less than inspiring. My wings had caught in the curtains and I'd tumbled off the platform, dragging half the stable with me. The whole audience laughed—and my stage fright was born. My dreams of stardom do not, by the way, include being a comedian. Romantic leads for me, or nothing.

The first-period bell rang, and the crowd of try-out hopefuls surged forward. I was half wishing I had been content to stay stagestruck in my dreams. "Nuts. I was nuts to even try this," I muttered. "I don't know why I'm even bothering to check the cast list."

Nevertheless I craned my neck a little higher to try to see over the heads of a couple of guys. "I'm just a glutton for punishment," I said glumly. "I probably flubbed the audition."

"*Flub* is not a word in Naomi Peters's vocabulary," Amanda piped up from beside me. She untangled herself from Max's arms. She and Max had become such an entwined, hand-holding sort of twosome these days, they were beginning to resemble a pretzel.

4

Amanda's cheeks were rosy with happiness, matching her pale-pink shirt. As she began to push forward toward the bulletin board, she looked exactly what I thought being in love should look like.

Not like me. Not like Josh. People in love looked a little blurry, and their minds were only on each other. My mind was on the play.

Josh's mind was on the second warning bell. As it jangled, he peered first at his watch, then at the clock over the lockers that were across from the auditorium. He looked at me and heaved a large sigh. It was not an in-love sort of sigh. It was more a let's-not-be-late-for-homeroom sort of sigh. Josh and I may have been dating for only a few months, but we have been buddies since grade five. Believe me. I know. It was definitely not an in-love sort of sigh.

Amanda let go of Max and squeezed in front of me and Josh. Amanda was short, and at the age of fifteen and a half had already learned how to elbow her way to the front of crowds. It was a skill I admired. "Coming through," she chirped, and the mob miraculously parted before her. I hung back a second, afraid people might notice me. Amanda simply grabbed the fringe on the sleeve of my new suede jacket and pulled me along in her wake. "Now, no more of this talk about flubbing things, Naomi," she scolded. "You have never flubbed anything in your life. You are terrific at everything you do. You are a budding Phi Beta Kappa."

5

"I'd rather be a budding Beauty, thank you."
That sounded so funny that Amanda and I shared
one of those crazy best-friends-since-kindergarten
looks and cracked up.

Max laughed with us. "I think Naomi is perfect
to play Beauty. . . ." He flashed me a grin and
poked up his glasses. I felt my face go red, but I
basked in his compliment. Everyone used to call me
Olive Oyl—I was that thin. But thankfully, I had
filled out a bit over the past year. "She's more than
pretty enough for the part," Max added.

"That's supposed to be your line," Amanda informed Josh.

"Line?" Josh raked his fingers through his short
sandy hair and looked confused. When he looks
like that, I do have an impulse to hug him, like you
would a slightly understuffed but friendly teddy
bear. Josh is a very sweet person, the perfect boy-
next-door. He's six feet two of freckles and broad
shoulders and the kind of friendly smile that makes
half the female population of our school do a double take when he strides down the hallways. One of
Josh's good points is he has no idea how attractive
he is to girls—most girls. I guess I've known him
too long to get weak-kneed when he's around.

After his weekly Monday-morning tennis match
with the tennis team, he was looking a little rumpled around the edges. But don't let the rumpled
edges fool you. Josh is the smartest kid in school.
He is president of the debating club, and has never

lost a tournament yet. And he's conning the extra-curricular committee to let him start a future-lawyers' club called Legal Eagles. But when it comes to human relations, he is always a little dazed and confused. It can be endearing—sometimes. "Uh—I missed something here," Josh said.

"You are her boyfriend," Amanda spelled it out. "And you are supposed to think she is so pretty there is no way anyone else in the world could be cast as Beauty."

"Of course I think you're pretty," Josh said to me, as if he was saying, I think the sky is blue, or, I think I'd like a sausage pizza for lunch. "But that's not how casting works," he added, ever the practical one. "And sure, it'd be great if you got the part, but it's not as if you wanted to be an actress or anything. C'mon, I think we're going to be late for class. And I can't afford to get Mr. Dunsmore upset."

I was upset, but I didn't have time to worry about it. Amanda was nose to nose with the bulletin board, and I was standing right behind her. We spotted my name at the exact same time. For a second the letters blurred and I felt like I was going to faint.

"You got it!" she shrieked.

"I got it," I whispered. My voice stuck in my throat. The blood drained from my face. "I got the lead. I don't believe it," I sort of croaked. My knees turned to Jell-O and I slumped against Amanda. "This is too good to be true!"

"Well, it *is* true." Amanda sounded so proud, I

7

straightened up and began to grin. She grinned back. "I *knew* you'd be good enough, but I didn't think a sophomore stood a chance. I'm glad, Naomi." Then she grabbed me and spun me around in a circle while Max pounded my back.

Josh gathered me from the whirlpool of Amanda and Max, and he squashed me in a big bear hug. His flannel shirt was soft against my skin, and I felt absolutely, completely happy.

Happiness, I've learned, is often a fleeting feeling. One minute you are high as Mt. Everest with joy, the next you plunge into the deepest ocean rift of despair. I used to worry about this. My mother says it has to do with being fifteen.

"Oh, ugh!" Amanda was frowning at the bulletin board. "Look who's playing the male lead."

Male lead. As in *the Beast.* How had I forgotten about the Beast? There is no Beauty without her Beast. But not once during tryouts yesterday had I thought about who'd be playing opposite me if I got the lead. All I had focused on was being Beauty—what she'd walk like, how she'd think, how her voice would sound. I tend to be a very single-minded sort of person. My parents, my friends, my teachers, think it is one of my outstanding qualities—perfect concentration.

"Bad news," she muttered. Then, "Yuck!"

"Yuck?" I repeated after Amanda. I didn't like her tone. It suggested something slimy, creepy—well, *beastlike.* I glanced down the hall at the retreating figures of some guys who had been checking out the cast list. Was one of them my leading man? None of them looked too awful to me. None of them looked like an "Oh, ugh." Or a "Yuck."

"Who *is* the leading man?" Max asked.

Josh wrenched his eyes away from his watch. "Leading man?"

"The play isn't just *Beauty*," I reminded him.

He frowned.

"Leading man, as in the Beast," I said patiently.

"I wouldn't call Dylan Russo a beast," Amanda said. "But I don't like his type. At least he's not shorter than you, Naomi."

"You know him?" Max sounded jealous.

Amanda beamed, and paused just long enough to give him a kiss.

"You are the only boy I *really* know. But there are guys I know *about*. . . ."

Dylan Russo. My imagination spun into high gear. Amanda knew "about" this guy. Bad sign. That meant he had a reputation of some kind. What if he was a total creep? And I'd have to *kiss* him, I realized for the first time. I'd have no choice.

"What exactly *do* you know about this guy Dylan?" Josh asked, putting a protective hand on my shoulder.

"His dad's Ray Russo, who runs the Double-R Repair and Fix-It Shop out in Keaton Corners," Amanda informed us.

9

My shoulders, my legs, my whole soul sagged with relief. A fix-it shop sounded so normal. Keaton Corners was a very normal place.

"Oh, that guy. The one with the Harley." Josh frowned. "I don't know him, but I saw him there when I brought my dad's snowblower in for repair last week."

"A biker? In a play? A leading man?" I tried to picture that.

"Weird, isn't it?" Amanda remarked.

"So why don't we know him?" Max asked, linking his hand in Amanda's. By now we were all hurrying down the hall toward our various homerooms.

"I heard he just transferred here in September. He was living in the Berkshires with his mom, and then he moved back here with his dad. Besides, he's a senior and he works at his dad's shop after school, so our paths wouldn't cross much."

"You're amazing. How do you know all this about someone you don't know?" Josh asked.

I answered for her. "Come off it, Josh. Amanda is Revere High's walking grapevine."

"The point is," Amanda said, linking arms with Max and quickening her step as the third and final bell rang, "he's not the sort of guy *I'd* like to kiss—"

"Glad to hear it!" Max mumbled into the curtain of Amanda's glossy red hair.

She extricated herself enough to add, "Let alone in all that beast makeup—yuck!"

"I don't like the idea of you kissing another guy

at all—beast makeup or not!" Josh said, taking my hand. It was a first. He never holds hands with me in school.

"You actually sound jealous," I teased, not sure how I felt about that. His hand tightened on mine, and I suddenly got this strange, closed-in sort of feeling.

"Don't worry, Josh—she won't like it. Not with Dylan Russo . . . beast makeup or not. I guarantee it!" Amanda said just as she and Max reached the turnoff for the west-wing homerooms.

"I wouldn't be so sure," I countered, feeling a little annoyed. For some reason my friends' attitudes were starting to get to me. Was I that boring? That predictable? Amanda didn't know everything about me. She had no idea I still read romances. Or that part of me considered Harleys very romantic. Or that all of me considered actors the stuff dreams are made of. "I might enjoy it!" I shot back, tossing my braid over my shoulder.

Amanda's eyebrows arched up. Max coughed. Josh looked like a hurt puppy. "Are you serious?"

"Josh . . ." I moaned. "Come off it. This is just a stage kiss we're talking about. Besides, I probably only kiss him once at the end—you know, to turn him into the prince of my dreams."

"Of your dreams?" Amanda burst out laughing, and elbowed Josh. "Don't worry, Josh. That'll be the day. Look, Naomi, you'll meet him in . . ." She checked her watch. "In exactly seven hours. You

11

can tell us all about this biker-actor phenom later. Let's celebrate after your rehearsal at Jonesy's. We'll meet you there." With that she waved a breezy good-bye, and she and Max broke into a half-run toward their classroom.

Josh actually stopped to peck me on the cheek right there in the hall—another first—then rushed into Mr. Dunsmore's class.

I raced down the opposite hall, vaguely annoyed with Amanda. What gave her the right to think she knew how I'd feel about kissing a guy—any guy? Maybe, for once in her life, Amanda would be wrong.

Chapter Two

SEVEN HOURS LATER Dylan Russo took me by surprise. He swung through the double doors of Revere High's Caudwell Theater twenty minutes late for the first cast call.

Every member of the cast and crew for *Beauty and the Beast* looked up. The houselights were on. We were gathered on the stage, sitting in a huge semicircle of chairs. Judi Bender, the drama coach, had just begun talking about the rehearsal schedule when Dylan finally waltzed in.

And just like everyone else who was already seated in the large circle of chairs on the stage, when Dylan Russo made his entrance, I leaned forward to get a better look.

He was handsome in a dark, catlike way—all cheekbones and eyes, and an angular face. He'd be great cast as a vampire. In spite of his dark hair and deep-brown eyes, he was fair. Actually, we had the same sort of coloring.

A motorcycle helmet with a red insignia was tucked under his arm. An earring glinted in his right ear. Lots of guys wear leather jackets and single earrings. Lots of guys I'd seen around school were even better looking. But something about Dylan made me stop and take notice. As if he was saying, "Hey, look at me. I'm here."

This guy had an effect on people. He certainly had an effect on me. He didn't make my heart throb, but he definitely made me very curious.

He was like a book with an eye-catching cover or title you just couldn't resist. I wanted to know everything about him.

Don't ask me why, but when I first glimpsed Dylan, I said a quick prayer that Amanda was wrong. That Dylan was not going to be bad news. He did sort of look like it, though. And I could see why she was worried about me kissing him.

"Thank you for turning up." Judi glanced over her clipboard.

"Some guy in my shop class had a problem with his car. I had to give him a lift to work." His voice was soft, but every word carried across the light buzz of conversation starting up among the rest of the cast and crew.

"The rehearsal was scheduled for three o'clock sharp," Judi said. She sat at one end of the semicircle of chairs, straddling her seat. As she talked, she punctuated her comments by tapping her clipboard against the back of the chair. I had known her for only twenty minutes, not counting yesterday's auditions, but I could see she was a person I wouldn't want to cross swords with. "I won't tolerate late entrances. I don't find them charming."

I thought Judi was being a little rough on the guy. Dylan didn't seemed fazed, though.

"I won't make a habit of it. But I couldn't let a guy lose his job, could I?"

Dylan Russo was beginning to impress me. I would have shriveled to the size of a dried pea if Judi or any other teacher ever talked to me that way.

"Right." Judi's tone softened a little. "And I admit it never hurt an actor to be a bit of a ham!" she added with a wink.

Everyone laughed. Dylan smiled. He didn't have a wide, grinny smile, the kind that Josh has. No, Dylan's smile just casually hung around his mouth.

He was still smiling as he headed for the only empty seat in the place. Next to me. "Hi," he said, shoving his helmet under the chair. "I'm Dylan. Dylan Russo. You must be Naomi."

I just stared at him. "Yeah . . ." I said slowly. "How did you know?"

As he took off his jacket, he tilted his head and considered my face. He was wearing a gray T-shirt with faded red lettering that read DOUBLE-R REPAIR AND FI -IT S OP. He was thin but muscular. He looked strong for his size. "You *are* my leading lady." He sat down and tugged at the frayed hole in the knee of his jeans. "Since you weren't already in the drama club, I asked around. I wanted to know who I'd be working with."

"Oh." He made it sound so sensible. Who he'd be *working* with. I felt very dumb. He hadn't been agonizing all day about exactly who Naomi Peters might be. Or if he'd like her. Or if she was some sort of creep. I wish I had thought to ask around more about him, too. Though I didn't know many seniors to ask.

Dave was passing out copies of the playbook. He handed one to Dylan and slapped him a high five. "Yo, Dylan," Dave said.

"Yo," Dylan said back.

Dylan fanned the pages of his playbook, then plunked it on the floor beside him. He looked at me. "Besides," he said, "haven't you noticed? Ever since the cast list went up this morning, everyone in this high school knows who we are."

"So that's why people have been staring at me?" I laughed this time. "I was trying to figure out if something was wrong with how I looked."

"No. Nothing's wrong with how you look." He said it plain and simple, and he wasn't flirting. Nothing like that. But I blushed anyway. If he noticed, he didn't let on. "In my old school, anyone who was cast in the play became an instant campus celebrity. Of course, Herman Melville High in the heart of the Berkshires wasn't half as big as this place."

16

"That's right. You're new in town. . . ."

"See, you know something about me, too." He leaned toward me and nudged me with his shoulder. His whole body seemed to radiate warmth and energy. It was a mildly unsettling feeling.

I pulled away from him and pretended to look offended, but I wasn't. "Not much, really. Just that you're a senior. That you ride a motorcycle and you started here in September."

He was about to say something else, but Judi started the rehearsal.

Judi asked a girl to pass around Xeroxes of the rehearsal schedule. The girl was short, and I had seen her in the halls. Her hair was spiky and dark, and she wore a sweatshirt that said MASQUES TECH CREW.

"Thanks, Marnie," Dylan said, taking a copy of the schedule and stretching out his legs. "Marnie, this is Naomi."

She smiled at me and winked at him.

And I wondered if they were dating.

"These are your schedules," Judi explained over the rustle of papers. "I want you to eat, sleep, and breathe them. Forget about the rest of your life for the next couple of weeks."

A girl next to me, who had introduced herself earlier as Dana, groaned. "In two weeks I'll be wondering for the zillionth time why I ever get involved in these plays. You'll see—they devour your life." Dana shook her head, and her huge earrings jangled. Her jeans were covered with colorful patches.

17

She'd told me she worked on costumes, which, somehow, considering her outfit, made sense.

"That's what's great about all this," Dylan commented from the other side of me. "I love loving something so much it devours you."

Before I had a chance to think about that, Judi glared in our direction and cleared her throat. "You have a week from today to have all your lines memorized."

My groan blended with two dozen others.

Out of the corner of my eye, I noticed Dylan looked glum. He caught my glance and made a face. "I am not a quick study. I'm lousy at memorizing."

"I'm a whiz at it," I told him. "I learned a couple of tricks from my third-grade teacher, Mrs. Bothwraithe."

"Bothwraithe?" He choked down a laugh. "Teach me some time. I could use some pointers."

"Sure." I shut up then, because Judi was once again glaring in our direction. I mentally reviewed my study schedule for the next few weeks. It would be hard to find time to coach him, but somehow I'd manage to fit it in.

"*As* I was saying . . ." Judi rapped her clipboard on the back of her chair again. "We've got just under three weeks to get our act together here. It sounds impossible, but it's more than possible. It's one week more than we had last spring for the year-end production."

"We're supposed to be grateful?" Marnie commented from across the semicircle. I noticed she was sitting next to a guy whose tech-crew sweat-shirt matched her own. She had one leg thrown over his. They gave off Max-and-Amanda sort of vibes. She obviously wasn't dating Dylan. I smiled at her and decided I liked her.

"To get started, we will do a series of acting exercises. They'll help you all loosen up. You'll begin to hone some acting skills, and you'll also get to know one another. We'll be working very closely and intensely these next few weeks. It'll be fun, mostly, but at times it gets tense, even crazy, and at the end, after the closing night, when this particular crew breaks up, you'll feel like you've lost all your best friends."

Dylan looked at me and I smiled what I hoped was a polite smile. I couldn't imagine becoming best friends with anyone so fast. I've known all my *best* friends—Amanda, Max, and Josh—since we were in grade school. Sure, I'd had lots of friends in school, but not the kind of people I'd share my deepest secrets with.

Judi moved to the center of the room. Her blond ponytail poked out from beneath a baseball cap. She was a thin, energetic woman, and I knew she still acted in New York on TV soaps occasionally. "Off your duffs, kids. Let's get in a circle and join hands."

Chairs scraped against the floorboards. The backdrops were raised high, and the stage stretched back into the gloom of the prop shop and storage areas. Everyone bumped one another. No one seemed eager to act like a bunch of kindergarten kids and make a circle holding hands. People joked about it.

First we played a couple of circle games I had almost forgotten how to play. Ring-around-the-rosy was one of them—if you can believe it. Then we did this bizarre thing where we all had to fall down on the floor and keep our eyes closed and play dead.

Next we did some yoga exercises so we could relax. When we all got up, Judi told us to pick a partner and imitate everything he or she did.

"Dylan," Judi said, "let's show them." She turned to the rest of us. "Dylan's had some professional training—he's done this before," she explained.

Everyone was watching them, laughing along as Dylan and Judi mirrored each other's actions. It seemed so silly. Then Judi made the rest of us join in. I held back, but Dana, my partner, started by skipping in a small circle like a little girl. I skipped too. I felt awkward, self-conscious; then I realized no one was watching me. Slowly I began to get a little looser. I made a funny face. Dana made the same face back. That made me laugh. She laughed back. She stuck her tongue out me. I stuck my tongue out at her.

"Change partners!" Judi shouted.

I found myself face-to-face with Dylan. He tilted his head to the left. I stood a moment, a little

confused. He patted his stomach and started rub
bing the crown of his head. I giggled and did th
same thing. Then he shouted. It wasn't a roar—i
was a yell that came straight from the bottom of hi
lungs. His eyes were challenging me. He didn'
know about my big, deep alto voice. I yelled back
He yelled louder. I yelled crazier. Then I took th
lead. I mustered up a huge shout. It soared right ou
of me. It felt wild and free and wonderful.

Dylan's mouth dropped open.

Shrieeek! Judi's whistle blew. "Stop!"

Everyone stopped instantly. My throat wa
pounding from the exertion. "That was awesome!'
I gasped.

The theater, the people in it, the drab walls, the
bright clothes, Marnie's spiky hair . . . the whole
world seemed alive with smells and colors and tex-
tures I'd never noticed before. I took a deep breath
but didn't close my eyes; I wanted to sop up ever
detail about this moment.

"You were great!" Dylan said as he staggered a
little against me. I slumped against him. "You're a
closet loudmouth!" he said, looking very impressed.
"I took you for the soft-spoken, quiet type."

"Fooled you!" I grinned up at him and we
sagged closer together. I was thinking I had fooled
myself, too. I had never shouted so loud before in
my life.

"Good, you two!" Judi had walked up to us. I
noticed that people who had worked through the

last exercise had sort of paired off. They were talking together, or sitting together, as if all the barriers between them had dropped. I suddenly loved everyone in the whole room.

"I want you to tell me exactly what you feel like. . . . No, Dylan, don't move—stay like that, leaning against Naomi. What do you feel like? First image that comes to your head."

I felt self-conscious, but I stayed there, though I was sure Dylan could feel my body tense.

He bit his lip and closed his eyes. I noticed his eyelashes were very long. "I feel—I feel like a broken column in one of those ancient Greek ruins," he said.

A picture of blue skies, white temples, and high hills filled my mind. "Me too."

"So then be columns, be ruins—trust each other. Lean," Judi told us.

I tried not to feel silly. Be a column? I tried. I leaned harder against him.

"Trust me," he said. "I won't let you fall."

I stiffened a little. I wasn't sure.

"Stand up now, Naomi," Judi told me.

I straightened up.

"Get behind her, Dylan. Naomi, fall back—he'll catch you."

"I can't do that. I'm scared of falling."

"Trust me," Dylan said again. He was behind me. I couldn't see him. Judi wouldn't let me turn around and see how far away he was. She just nodded encouragement.

22

"Sag!" she ordered.

I sagged straight back. I fell so far, I almost screamed. Then Dylan's arms caught me when I was only a foot off the floor. His grasp was sure and tight, and I felt his heart pounding. His strength seemed to flow right into me through my back. Then he helped me straighten up again, and turned me to face him.

That's when I realized we were the exact same height. My eyes were level with his eyes.

It was at least three seconds before I realized we were still looking at each other. I pulled away, and that's when I blushed.

Judi blew her whistle.

"I told you that you could trust me," he murmured as Judi gave us a few last instructions about lines and schedules and practice.

I don't think I heard a word she said.

When the rehearsal broke up, Dylan retrieved his bike helmet from beneath the chair. He hung back a little as the crowd filed down the theater aisles. "I don't believe you've never done this before," Dylan said as he put on his jacket. I noticed a small tattoo on the back of his left hand. I wondered if it was the wash-off kind. Somehow I doubted it.

I shook my head. I realized he was hanging back so he could talk to me. I felt flattered. And a little confused.

"You're a natural. Some of that stuff you were doing while I was copying your movements, those big, broad gestures. On stage they'd really carry. People in the back row would really understand what you're feeling. You're very good, Naomi."

"Not as good as you," I hurried to point out.

"I've acted professionally. . . ."

"So Judi said." I wasn't sure if what was so good about Dylan had anything to do with being a pro or not. But I was sure that after one afternoon of crazy theater exercises, I ached to be as good as he was. On impulse I bargained, "I'll teach you to memorize, if you teach me some of your acting techniques."

His smile brightened, and he took my hand to shake it. "It's a deal!"

Suddenly, outside of the safety of the rehearsal and the acting exercises, touching him felt too intimate.

I pulled away and held my books in front of my chest. I wrapped my arms around them and held on for dear life.

"I'm new here, and working together is an easy way to make friends," he said, digging at a crack in the floor with the heel of his boot. He looked a little lonely.

"Of course," I replied. I felt a little guilty. I had forgotten about Dylan being new. I felt as if I had known him a long time already.

The four-thirty bell rang. Dylan jumped a little. "I gotta go," he said, snapping up his jacket.

24

"Me too," I said. I had to go to my locker and get the rest of my books.

"See ya later." Dylan smiled at me and gave a little self-conscious shrug. Then he turned on his heel and half sprinted out the side door.

I stood a moment longer, watching the door close behind him. *Wait until I tell Amanda that Dylan's not a beast.* Just touching Dylan, being next to him, had been a very interesting experience. I couldn't imagine what it would be like kissing him.

Or could I? I wondered as I jogged toward my locker.

Chapter Three

I WAS STANDING on the sidewalk outside of school, waiting for the light to change. My cowboy boots were firmly planted on the cement, but I felt like I was hovering a good six inches over the pavement. What a great day this had been!

Then I saw Josh waving at me from the window of Jonesy's, across the way. Amanda was there too, leaning over his shoulder. I couldn't see Max, but his Jeep was parked in front. Everyone had waited for me.

"Yo! Naomi!" The cry behind me was almost drowned out by the roar of an engine.

I turned around. There, on a big black Harley, was Dylan. Even with his helmet down and his jacket zipped up, I recognized him. He had pulled out of the traffic lane and onto the shoulder of the road. He gunned the motor a couple of times.

The smell of the exhaust made me cough.

I liked the way "Yo" sounded. I tried saying it. "Oh—yo. Nice bike," I shouted over the noise of the motor and traffic.

"Want a ride?" he offered.

I gasped. "On that?" What girl hasn't dreamed of riding off into the sunset with a cool-looking guy wearing a leather jacket and an earring? But deep down I'm actually scared of motorcycles. My dad is the head emergency-room surgeon at Revere General Hospital, and he has a poor opinion of them; he says they kill people or maim them for life.

Besides, Amanda, Max, and Josh were right across the way, looking out of Jonesy's front window, waiting for me.

"I can't."

Dylan's smile faded. "I thought maybe you lived somewhere on the way to Keaton Corners. . . ."

"I don't. . . . I mean, I live that way." I felt so dumb. I pointed down South Chestnut toward Old Town Road. "But I'm meeting friends." I nodded toward Jonesy's. The old renovated fifties diner shone in the silvery afternoon light. *Dylan should get to know this place,* I thought, *if he's going to fit in around here. If we're going to be friends.*

"Oh," he said, as he settled his helmet back on his head. And for the second time that afternoon I got the impression he was lonely.

I reached out and touched his arm. "Hey, why don't you come and join us. . . . Have you been to

27

Jonesy's?" I knew he didn't hang out there regularly, or I would have known who he was.

"Only once. Last week. To pick up the jukebox for repair," he said, then noticed the three faces staring at me out the window. "Your friends are waiting. . . ." he added with a small smile. "But thanks for asking. Some other time. Gotta get to work now."

He didn't actually mention that he worked at his dad's shop. I wondered if he was embarrassed about doing manual work or something. None of my friends had jobs after school, though Amanda and I occasionally baby-sat for family friends. I also wondered what Josh and company were thinking as they watched me talk to this guy on a Harley.

"See you," I said, hugging my books hard.

He let up his brake and revved his engine. Just before he pulled back into traffic, Dylan called over his shoulder. "Don't forget—you owe me one of Mrs. Bothwraithe's memorizing lessons." He gunned his engine again. "Okay if I call you about it?"

"Yeah," I said, laughing, as he buzzed off up the road to Keaton Corners. "My phone number . . . we're not listed!" I yelled after him. But he was too far gone to hear me. I watched the Harley weave in and out of traffic, until I lost sight of it around a curve. Then I remembered the cast and crew of *Beauty and the Beast* had their phone numbers listed on the schedules Judi handed out. I even had Dylan's.

I heard the traffic signal click. The light was green. I raced across the street and took the front steps to the diner two at a time.

"Hi, guys!" I gasped, hanging up my jacket on one of the little hooks on the side of the booth. Max got up and let me slide in past him. We always sat like that. Me next to Max, across from Josh. Amanda next to Josh, across from Max.

I collapsed in the fake-leather seat and slid down until my chin was even with the table. The Formica was turquoise with a black diamond pattern. I ran my finger over the surface and grinned at Josh across the way. Then at Amanda. I wanted to hug everybody. I felt silly and energized and very breathless.

"I told you so!" Amanda chanted in a singsong voice. "He's a biker."

My jaw dropped. "So?"

"Hard to picture you working with someone like that, Naomi. He looks a little tough," Max remarked.

I straightened up in my seat. "He is a little tough. What's wrong with that? He can still act."

Amanda was looking at me like I was a new arrival from Pluto or something.

"For a minute I thought you were going to ask him to come in here with you," Josh said, sounding miffed. He stared at me. "You look different." His tone shifted from miffed to perplexed.

I caught a sort of funhouse reflection of myself in the chrome side of the napkin holder. My hair

29

had worked loose from my braid, and my cheeks were pink.

I looked across the table at Josh and realized I had to look up slightly. Dylan and I were the same height. We looked at each other eye to eye. "I feel different," I stated. Ever since rehearsal ended, I'd felt alive and new. I felt that every second every bit of me was changing. "I feel different, Josh. I've just tried something new and wonderful. . . ." But I felt too impatient to explain it all right then. And I couldn't let Amanda get away with what she'd just said about Dylan and his Harley. She made *biker* sound like a dirty word.

"He does ride a Harley, Amanda. You knew that. Bikers aren't necessarily criminals."

Amanda made a calming motion with her hands. "Okay, okay. What are you so worked up about, anyway?" She leaned back to let the waitress put a diet soda in front of her. Amanda daintily squeezed the lemon over the mound of ice cubes. I detest ice in soda. Amanda thrives on it. She took a sip. "You barely know the guy. Most guys I see riding Harleys hang out at Pulito's."

"Dylan's not at all like those guys," I insisted, hoping he didn't hang out with the Pulito's crowd. They were a pretty rough bunch. "But he *is* a real actor. I'll tell you that much." My annoyance with Amanda dissolved as I began to fill everyone in on the rehearsal.

"It sounds like fun," Amanda conceded. I could

tell she was trying to be enthusiastic, but she looked a little skeptical. "Just sounds pretty demanding."

"Especially during midterms. Don't you have a big paper coming up for American history? Amanda does," Max said, stretching his arms above his head. He ordered another cup of coffee. Max is the only sixteen-year-old I know who practically inhales coffee—the heavy-duty, real-caffeine kind.

Midterms. Grades. That dumb history paper. I felt the blood drain from my face, and my stomach clenched. The paper was due the same day I was supposed to have all my lines memorized for the play. "Yeah, I do. Midterms were the furthest thing from my mind when I tried out for the play."

"Naomi, the homework queen of the sophomore class?" Amanda remarked with a startled laugh. "Forgot about *midterms*!"

"I don't know about this play stuff, Naomi. . . . It's not like you to space out about school like this." Josh frowned at me. "Didn't you realize it would take half your time?"

"Nope." I was beginning to feel pretty stupid. How could I have forgotten about schoolwork? This certainly was becoming a week of firsts for me—first impulsive thing I'd ever really done in my life. First lead in the first play I ever tried out for. First rehearsal. First new friend in ages. But I was beginning to fear all these new firsts were going to lead to my first *F*!

"Hey, cheer up. It's not the end of the

world," Max added. "You'll manage it all."

"You always do, Naomi," Amanda concurred. "After all, you were voted most likely to be Phi Beta Kappa in Mr. Blaustein's homeroom."

"I hope so," I said. But today my mind hadn't been on Phi Beta anything. It had been on learning to let myself go.

Just thinking about how great the afternoon had been, I didn't want to worry about midterms yet. Midterms could wait until I got home and hit the books. Meanwhile I wanted to savor the magic a little longer. I wanted Amanda, Josh, and Max to understand how great it all had been.

"Still," I continued, "just getting cast as Beauty makes me feel so good. Like I finally really and truly accomplished something on my own."

"Winning first prize in the county science fair two years running isn't accomplishing something?" Josh asked. He had been my science partner one year, Amanda the other.

"Of course it counts . . . but I'm *used* to being smart. I'm not used to being—well, talented or artistic or pretty." The last word popped out, and I felt myself blush.

Amanda reached over and tugged my braid. "You are pretty. But Harvard Law School won't be looking at your face. They're focused on law boards and transcripts."

"Give her a break. We haven't even gotten through high school yet," Max said. This was one of our crowd's running arguments. Amanda and Josh had this thing about planning every detail of our futures. They'd even figured we'd all be partners in the same Boston law firm together: Zukowski, Davidson, Munoz, and Peters. Max wasn't quite as convinced what his life would hold after college. And after today, neither was I.

I changed my mind all the time. Some days I wanted to be a doctor. To take life and death into my own hands and somehow make a difference. Then the law bug would bite me again, or I'd think of being the country's first woman president. Whatever I did, I wanted it to be challenging. Something not everyone could do.

And today I was feeling maybe I wanted to act.

The thought petrified me. It seemed ridiculous.

More ridiculous was the thought of how I'd get all my homework done. Studying for biology midterms and writing my history paper—not being an actress—were reality right now. So were grades. So was learning all those lines by next week. My heart sank. "Who am I kidding?" I sighed. "Maybe I bit off more than I can chew here . . . but—"

"You can't back off now!" Josh looked horrified. "You made a commitment. You're in the play, and you're going to do a great job at being Snow White—"

"Beauty!" Max, Amanda, and I shouted at once. I wanted to kill him for not remembering something so important, but I started to laugh. Leave it to Josh not to get his fairy tales straight.

"Right. Beauty, whatever." Josh looked annoyed. "You can do it—if anyone can. And then it'll be out of your system."

"Out of my system?" I was barely able to repeat the words. A person gets the flu out of her system. Or a passion for wearing only pale green. Or a crush.

"Maybe acting is something I don't want to get out of my system," I said finally. "Why should I? Maybe it's part of who I really am."

"Since when?" scoffed Amanda.

Josh lifted his eyebrows.

Max smiled at me.

"I'm serious," I said.

"After one play rehearsal she's serious about acting. Get real, Naomi," Amanda said. "Enjoy the experience, then move on. Isn't that one of the reasons you tried out for the play? To *try* new things. Not to get hooked on the first thing you try."

One of the reasons, Amanda, I said to myself. But I wasn't going to explain right then about that Christmas pageant, and my secret passion for stardom.

"Next thing you know, you'll be applying to Yale for acting school," Max suggested.

"Don't start giving her ideas!" Josh exclaimed. "Last I heard we were all going to Harvard Law School. Right, Naomi?"

I didn't answer. Suddenly I didn't want to know

what I was going to do after college. I didn't even want to know where I was going to college. Above all I didn't want to feel boxed in. This whole conversation was making me feel like the windows inside me that had been flung open during rehearsal were being shut again. "Gimme a break, Josh—I'm just a sophomore. I don't have to think about this yet."

"I've known you since you were nine years old, and you always planned to go to Harvard and become something," Josh grumbled, grabbing the check.

"I'm still going to become something," I snapped. "I just don't know what yet. I'm only fifteen, Josh. My life hasn't even begun." *Or has it?* I thought, following Max out of the booth.

"Touchy, touchy!" Amanda teased. "What's wrong with you today?" she asked more seriously as we headed out of the diner while the boys hung back to pay.

"Nothing, Amanda," I replied, hurt that she didn't understand. Something wonderful had happened to me today, and my friends just didn't get it.

Journals are what friends can't ever be. A diary is a true-blue friend you can always confide in.

That night, with my radio tuned to a late-night jazz station and my knees drawn up under my purple down quilt, I bared my soul to my journal. I filled three whole pages with my tiny writing, just talking about the day and Dylan and how it felt to have a chance to make a dream come true.

Most of all I wrote about how much fun I'd had playing those silly games, trusting another person enough to fall back into his arms. Of course, not just any person's arms. Dylan's arms. The thought was sweet for all of a second. After I wrote that, I chewed my pencil, stared at the yellow flowered wallpaper above the white wainscoting in my room, and sighed.

The sigh melted into a distinct pang of guilt and a vague sense of confusion.

Writing so much about the play and Dylan made me think about Josh. I sometimes wondered why I ever began dating him. I tried to list the reasons:

1. We are both tall. I'm the tallest girl in the sophomore class. He's one of the tallest juniors. Basketball coaches have drooled over us ever since junior high. Not much to base a relationship on, except that we both *hate* basketball.

2. We used to live next door to each other, before Josh's parents moved to the fancy new subdivision just east of Keaton Corners last year. So we've known each other forever.

3. We were leftovers. The day-old meat loaf of our crowd, Josh always says. Amanda, Max, Josh, me, and a couple of other kids who've since moved away have always hung out together. At thirteen we all sort of began to group date. As soon as Max got his license, he and Amanda suddenly paired off and started going everywhere . . . *alone* . . . in his Jeep. That left me and Josh, and two do not a group date make.

By our third time at the movies, just the two of us, Josh held my hand. It was the latest Teenage Mutant Ninja Turtles flick, and I remember every bit of it. Holding hands didn't erase every thought in my head or fill my tummy with butterflies. Nothing like that. It was a very nice, familiar sort of feeling. No rockets blasted, no fireworks went off, but I liked cuddling him.

It was the same sort of warm, home-baked apple-pie sensation later that same night when he kissed me good night at the door. We were both a little embarrassed about it. Our noses bumped, and we giggled afterward. We've kissed more since, but not one of Josh's kisses has ever sent me into orbit.

I had just finished writing this when the phone rang. My reaction was not to run for the phone—I'm not allowed to have my own phone until my sixteenth birthday—but to look at my alarm clock. It was 11:35 P.M. Everyone who knows me knows I can't have phone calls past ten thirty on school nights.

So I figured it wasn't for me. I let it ring again, closed my journal, sank back under my quilt, and patted my red cat Pebbles until he purred. Funny how Josh made me think of apple pie, and Dylan . . . Dylan made me stop thinking. Or made me think only of him.

"Naomi, it's for you!" my mother yelled a moment later. She did not sound happy about that.

I sat up straight. "Me?" Who'd be calling me now?

I hopped out of bed and rushed into the hall. I didn't bother with my robe or slippers. My mother had come in late from work and was still dressed in her business suit. Downstairs the TV was on.

"It's someone from that theater club," she said, handing me the receiver. She took off her jacket and undid the tiny silver cuff links in her silk blouse. She looked a little tired as she headed for the bedroom. "I don't know who's calling you this late," she added, with more than a trace of annoyance in her voice.

I had no idea either, but I wished she didn't look so upset. I waited for her to close the door to her room. I took my hand off the receiver. "Hi," I said.

"Uh—Naomi?"

I'd know that voice anywhere.

"Dylan?" I half breathed his name. I leaned back against the wall and tucked one foot up under my nightgown.

"I didn't think it was that late. . . ."

I suddenly felt very fifteen, very young. He *was* a senior, after all. "House rules. No calls past ten thirty on school nights." I had to tell him, in case he called again. I started to grin. Maybe he really would call again.

"I got to thinking . . ."

"About?"

"About Mrs. Bothwraithe."

I felt a little let down. "Oh. Our memorizing lessons."

"I knew it was late and all, but I didn't think—"

"No. No. It's okay." I didn't want him to hang up. I was listening to hear the sounds of his house in the background. There was music playing. He was listening to the same late-night jazz station I was.

I wondered what his house was like. I tried to picture where the phone was and decided it was in the kitchen. I imagined his kitchen yellow and bright, the color of sunflowers. I could picture him leaning against the kitchen counter, talking to me.

I sat down and curled my toes in the thick pile of the rug. "So what about Mrs. Bothwraithe?"

"We have so little time to learn these lines. Good thing *you're* a quick study," he said. "You're in almost every scene. I just have to beast around and brood a lot." He made a growly sort of sound.

I threw back my head and laughed.

He laughed with me. "But I still have enough to learn. I thought I should get started."

"Right." I tried to remember my schedule. The one I had worked out this afternoon during rehearsal.

"Maybe you could give me pointers now . . . at least get me started."

"Now? On the phone?" I heard the disappointment in my own voice.

"It *is* late. I guess I'd better wait."

"No," I practically shouted back into the receiver. "We can start right now." I paused to collect my thoughts. "First of all, she said to take small bits of what you have to learn and sing them to yourself."

"Sing?"

"Right. Like the way little kids do when they are learning the alphabet. It helps somehow. But most important, take a group of lines, half a scene, whatever, and read it before you go to sleep. Then say it again and again until you fall asleep with it running through your head. . . . You'll wake up remembering them."

"Really?"

"Trust me!" I said, in the exact same tone of voice he had used with me at the rehearsal today.

We both laughed. "I just may do that!" Dylan said.

There was a pause. I didn't want to hang up. I don't think he was in much of a rush to say good-bye either.

"Well . . . it is late. . . ." he finally said. His voice had dropped a little lower.

"Right . . . I have to go."

"Right . . . tomorrow . . ."

"Sure." We both hung up, but neither of us said good-bye.

I stretched out my legs straight in front of me and sat on the floor with the phone on my lap. I don't know how long I stayed there. I couldn't stop thinking how it felt to talk to a guy you'd just met and never wanted to say good-bye to.

"Naomi?" My mother had come out of her room. She had on her bathrobe and was brushing her hair. "Who was that on the phone?"

Something in her voice warned me off. "You mean who called just now?"

"Right." She looked down at me sitting on the floor.

I got up and smiled what I hoped was a very casual smile. "Oh, that was Dylan. Dylan Russo. He's the guy who got cast in the role of the Beast."

"Figures . . ." my mother said, still not looking very pleased.

"But I forgot," I said casually. "You weren't here for dinner. You don't know." I couldn't control my smile anymore. "I got the lead part. I'm playing Beauty!"

My mother's eyes widened. "Hey, that's great!" she said. "But I hope being in a play won't interfere with schoolwork. Don't get too wrapped up in this theater business. It's going to take a lot of your time. And rehearsals can get pretty demanding."

"Tell me about it!"

"But this boy . . . what's his name?"

"Dylan," I said carefully. My mother *never* forgets a name.

"Why is he calling so late? He'd better not make a habit of it. How well do you know him?"

"Oh, Mom," I cried. "Don't look so worried. He won't call this late again. He wanted to work out some rehearsal stuff. We'll have to be rehearsing pretty closely together. He *is* my leading man, after all." Something in my mother's face made me decide it was best not to say more.

41

"As long as he knows the house rules," she said. She started down the stairs and turned back. "I can't say I like the way he sounded on the phone. He's not as polite as Josh."

I sighed. "Look, Mom, Dylan's okay—really he is. If he weren't, would Judi Bender have cast him in the play? You know she's a very tough drama teacher."

"Well, he doesn't sound like your usual friends, that's all," she said. She pursed her lips slightly and looked a bit worried. She stared at me a second, then headed down the steps.

"He's not like them. No. Not at all," I answered back, but in a soft voice so she really couldn't hear me.

Chapter Four

"WHY DON'T YOU let your hair down, Naomi?" Judi asked from her front-row seat in the theater early the next week.

I looked up from my script, confused.

Judi laughed. "Yes, get rid of that braid. You always have your hair pulled back or up in a ponytail. C'mon, shake it loose. See how it feels." Judi sat back and watched me struggle with the tightly wound scrunchie. I felt self-conscious. But I obeyed her, even though I already knew what my hair felt like loose. A mess.

I leaned forward and let my hair curtain my eyes. Then I straightened up, shook my head, and saw Dylan looking at me from the wings.

"Nice!" he said in a stage whisper, pointing to my hair.

I laughed, touching my hair, and felt my face grow warm.

"That's more like it!" Judi said. "Now you look like a girl about to fall in love." Judi hopped up on the stage and eyed me critically. "From now on, wear a long skirt when we rehearse, just to get used to moving around the set in a skirt. In fairy tales girls don't wear jeans. Your costume will help you find your character."

Then Judi told Andrea to clear the stage so she could rehearse the next scheduled scene, the Prologue. It was between Dave, who played Beauty's father, and Dylan. It was the morning after the Beast sheltered Beauty's father from the storm.

I grabbed my sweater and script and sat behind Judi. I needed to work on my lines, but I longed to watch Dylan. Dave and I had one more run-through scheduled a little later, so I had the perfect excuse to hang around.

Of course, Dylan had no beast makeup yet. He wasn't even wearing the mask Judi had told him to buy yesterday for practice. He was wearing loose black sweatpants and a black hooded sweatshirt. He wore a pair of soft old sneakers.

I wondered if changing from jeans and biker boots to sweats and sneakers before practice was his way of getting into his character. I decided to ask him later.

Dylan took the stage. He pulled up the hood of his sweatshirt and turned his back on everyone for a moment. His whole body tensed with concentration. He seemed like a panther about to pounce on something. Then he flipped down his hood again and turned around. Everyone in the audience gasped.

I hardly recognized Dylan. His face looked creepy. Like someone you wouldn't want to meet alone on a dark street. He had an angry, pained expression on his face.

You could feel his hurt and fear from the tenth row.

Throughout the scene Dylan's voice was menacing. He curled his shoulders in on himself and looked like a wounded, angry cat. I was caught in the web of fantasy Dylan was spinning right in front of my eyes.

When the scene ended, there was a split second where Dylan was still the Beast. Then the role seemed to slip off him like water, and the guy standing on the stage was a seventeen-year-old high-school kid, looking hopefully at Judi for a comment. No, not just a comment. Every atom of Dylan's body seemed to ache for praise.

The theater was silent for a moment; then Judi actually clapped. So did everyone else. "That was incredible, Russo," Dave said.

Dylan shoved his fists in the front pocket of his sweatshirt and colored with pleasure.

Judi went back up on stage and gave some pointers to the guys. I strained forward in my chair to hear what she had to say. Dylan's performance had inspired me. I was determined to know everything in the world there was to know about acting, about theater, about creating a character.

A little later, during a break, Dylan offered to show me around the theater. "I can't believe you've never explored this place." His dark eyes were shining as he led me out the door at the front of the side aisle. I had been backstage once last week, to have Dana fit my costumes and to work a little with Judi. I had even joked with Dana about the one long dressing room—the girl members of the cast got to use it. The boys had to change in the men's bathroom.

We headed toward the room where props and scenery were stored. We could still hear Judi giving lighting pointers. We also heard hammering and voices from the theater shop as the stagehands constructed sets.

I followed him into the prop room. Racks of old costumes lined one wall. Dusty panels of scenery leaned against the other walls. Swords, hats of every shape and color, bolts of faded fabric poked out of baskets. A single low-watt lightbulb dangled from the ceiling, casting eerie shadows on everything. It looked a little like Phantomland in our local amusement park.

I wandered over toward a spindly-legged dressing table with a big oval mirror. The glass was so dirty, I couldn't see myself. With my finger on the dirty mirror I wrote NAOMI=BEAUTY and the year. Then, on impulse, I added DYLAN=BEAST.

"Hey, look at this!" Dylan said. I cleared off a bigger patch of mirror and erased our names. Dylan's reflection shone back at me. He had found a big plumed hat. He plopped it on his head, struck a pose, and drooped into a deep, gallant bow. Then he grabbed a sword and began fencing with a make-believe foe.

He snared a dusty red-velvet cloak off a hanger and tossed it to me. Draping it over my shoulders, I peeked in the mirror and was half surprised to see my hair was still down. I flipped it over the stiff stand-up collar.

I suddenly felt silly, like I was six years old. But alone with Dylan, I also felt very grown up. I turned to him. I wanted him to understand. "You know what this place reminds me of?"

He poked the end of his sword into the wooden floor. "An attic."

"In an old house! Playing dress-up and make-believe."

"So that's why we have so much in common," Dylan said.

"What's why?"

"Attics, make-believe. See, you are a born ac-tress. Tell me you don't love it. Isn't Judi right? Just by letting your hair down and putting on a cos-tume, you can be a whole different person."

"I never thought of that before—that acting was like playing in the attic. But it is." Then I told him how being a star of stage and screen someday had been one of my most cherished secrets.

"Not going to stay a secret for long. . . . I bet Beauty's just the first role you get here. You're only a sophomore, Naomi. And you're talented. You've got a lot to learn, but you're a natural." Then he told me about this book by a Russian guy that was all about how to create a character. He said I should read it. While he talked, he was fiddling with some stuff in a basket. "Hey, look at this!" He handed me a gilded hand mirror and a matching long-handled hairbrush. It was the kind I'd seen in vintage movies.

I tested the brush and began running it through my hair. Dylan sat on one end of the dressing table, watching me. As he watched, he talked in a soft voice. "I have my dreams too, Naomi. I don't just want to act. . . . Someday I want to direct plays."

He got up and stretched his arms high, giving an impatient shake of his head. "The problem is I want it all."

I stopped brushing my hair and considered his reflection. He looked pent up, excited, eager—and something else. Afraid? I realized then he wasn't quite as sure of himself as he seemed. "Hey, Dylan . . ." I said. "I don't know much about theater. But if I had a million dollars to bet, I'd bet you will have it all."

He met my glance in the mirror. "You mean that?"

"I mean it." And I did. "In fact, I bet Yale

48

would even give you a scholarship. I hear they have a great drama department. You're that good."

"*Yale?*" He stared at me as if I'd grown an extra nose or something. "Forget it. Who wants to go to Yale?"

"You don't?"

Dylan strode back over toward me and crouched down near the trunk, resting his hands on the curved wooden lid. "Yale? School? That's not where acting's at. No way. I want the real thing. I can't put off my life for four years while I get some dumb acting degree. I want to live theater. Breathe it. After graduation I'm outta here. I'm heading for New York—"

"Broadway?"

"Sure." He got up and paced the floor behind me. His eyes were shining as he spoke. "Or off-Broadway, or who-cares-what little theater. I just want to make real art. School—that's okay for some stuff, like becoming a teacher or a scientist. But to act—to really act—you've got to really live."

"But how will you manage in a place like New York?"

"Who knows?" he said carelessly. "I'll figure something out. I've always managed somehow. I'm pretty handy, and I can work hard at almost any sort of job. As long as I get a chance to work in real theaters, I don't care what else I do or how much money I make."

I swallowed hard. It was almost too much to

take in. I had never thought about life like this before. That you could want to do something big
with your life without necessarily going to school. I
had always thought of college as a pretty exciting
place. But Dylan made it sound—I don't know—
kind of uninteresting. Or at least not as exciting as
the life he pictured for himself.

I started tugging the brush through my hair
again. As usual it was tangled, and brushing hard
yanked at my scalp. It hurt.

"Don't do that," Dylan said. He had a funny
catch in his voice. Then, before I knew what was
happening, he had taken the brush from my hands.

I laughed, but my heart started beating faster.
He touched my hair so gently; then he started
brushing it. I was surprised it didn't hurt.

He met my glance in the mirror with a look in
his eyes that made my whole spine turn to mush. If
I hadn't been sitting down, I think I would have
fainted right then and there. He reached down and
settled the red cloak back on my shoulders, then
fanned my hair over it. He bent his head low over
mine . . .

"Break's over!" Dave Martin's voice boomed
suddenly.. He was someplace outside the prop
room, but very nearby.

Dylan jumped back.

I jumped up and almost hit him in the chin with
my shoulder. His hand reached out to steady me.
For a moment our fingers locked together. For one

second I wanted to stay that way forever. The next second I wondered exactly what in the world I was thinking. I pulled my hand away and began to re-fold the cloak.

"Peters, Russo, where are you guys?"

"Here!" Dylan actually sounded casual, as if nothing had almost happened between us.

"On stage now!" Dave walked into the prop room and looked at us. Dylan had glided over to the sword basket, and he looked up at Dave with a broad, friendly grin.

I was standing in the shadows. I felt as red as my cloak, but Dave didn't seem to notice. He cornered Dylan and began talking.

"So what do you think of this place?"

"Great. I was just telling Naomi about how ter-rific this theater is. Actually, I was wondering," Dylan continued in a friendly, matter-of-fact voice, "do you have theater books here? Like Stanislavski . . ."

"Who?"

"Stanislavski. It's called *Building a Character*. Do you have that one? I thought Naomi should read it sometime."

Dave shook his head. "Try the school library," he said as he angled his big shoulders through the doorway.

Dylan followed a step or two, then turned to me. "Hey, Naomi, I have it at home. Why don't you come over to my place after rehearsal and bor-row it?"

51

"Today?" It was the first word I said. And my usually deep voice sort of squeaked. I felt my face go from pale to red to pale again. It was like a code. Dylan was telling me, *Yes, something almost just happened. I don't want this moment to end.* I lost my voice for a moment and couldn't meet his eyes. I had almost kissed this guy right there in the prop room, and now I had to act, *we* had to act, as if nothing at all had happened.

"I can't. I have to baby-sit as soon as I leave here."

"Some other time, then."

Dave broke in. "Hey, I'd like to see it too . . . maybe when Naomi's done with it." We were in the wings by now. Dave stopped and stared at me. Marnie was doing something to the lights, and for a second one was aimed full at me. "Wow, Naomi. You look—you look beautiful," Dave said with a self-conscious little grin.

"She's supposed to." Dylan clapped him on the back and winked at me. "After all, she is Beauty!"

He sauntered off with Dave. I trailed behind them, half grateful for a minute to pull myself together. And half confused. What had almost happened back there in the prop room? First Dylan almost kissed me, and now, a heartbeat later, he's talking shop with Dave. He sure could switch gears fast. One second he's all intense about his future as an actor, the next he's all intense about me, and barely a minute later he's acting as if nothing at all was going on between us. It was enough to make me wonder if what had just happened was real, or make-believe like the play. Dylan could slip in and out of moods so fast—from biker to actor to repairman to boyfriend. As I tried to catch my breath, I began to wonder who or what the real Dylan was.

Thank goodness Sharon Jane Smithson is a sweet, sleepy baby. I usually do homework when I baby-sit. But just as my life had changed since getting the lead in the play, so had my normal baby-sitting routine. Last week was spent memorizing lines while Sharon Jane slept. This week I found myself writing in my journal about how incredible it felt to wear my hair down. Who had time for homework anymore?

The doorbell rang, and I jumped. Then I got up quickly, slammed the journal shut, and put my biology textbook on top of it. I raced to the front door before the bell rang again and woke up Sharon Jane.

"Amanda!"

"Don't look so surprised," she said as she pushed by me with a grin. Max followed behind her, and then Josh. "We knew you'd be here tonight—as usual. So since midterms are over for all of us, we thought we'd drop in."

"To celebrate," Josh contributed.

Max, who has a one-year-old baby sister, put his finger to his lips. "Quietly, of course."

I wanted to hug Max for that. I led everyone into the family room, away from the desk. Away from my journal.

One great thing about the Smithsons: They believe teenage baby-sitters should be treated with dignity and respect. And most important: They should be fed. The Smithsons stock their refrigerator with snacks, leave a whole box of microwave popcorn on the counter, and make it clear it's fine if I have friends over while Sharon Jane sleeps. As long as we keep it all down to a low roar, clean up the dishes, and don't make a major party of it.

Amanda and I sent the boys off to the kitchen. Amanda is a firm believer that men should microwave. They should also learn to wash dishes, do laundry, and change diapers. At the Smithsons', microwaving is about all Max and Josh can muster up.

Alone in the living room, Amanda noticed the brush I'd bought on my way here. As soon as Sharon Jane had winked off, I'd spent twenty whole minutes brushing my hair. Just to remember what it felt like when Dylan did it.

Then I had started writing in my journal.

"You're wearing your hair down," Amanda commented. She paused, looking at the brush. "That's new." She picked it up and slid it through her long, silky hair. Amanda always wears her hair down.

At that moment part of me longed to tell her everything . . . how it felt to watch Dylan act. How alive he was. How he knew everything there was to know about theater. How I had never met anyone like him. How gentle his hands were when he'd brushed my hair.

My cheeks burned at the thought. I couldn't tell Amanda anything. She didn't like Dylan. She thought I should love Josh.

"I haven't seen your hair down for ages," she said, stepping back. She tossed the brush on the sofa, hooked her fingers in the belt loops of her jeans, and eyed me. She nodded. "I like it. It looks different . . . but how come the change now?"

Inside, I was squirming. I felt as if I had a neon sign flashing right across my forehead: DYLAN=CHANGE.

I gulped and thought quickly. "The role . . . Judi suggested I see what it feels like to wear it down," I said truthfully. "Fairy-tale heroines always wear their hair down."

Amanda laughed heartily. "Right." She flopped down on the nearest chair and shook her head. "Remember when we were about seven and you decided to let your hair grow until it reached your feet, so you could be a princess?"

"I said that?"

"Yup, and that you would never ever cut it. And actually, you've barely cut it since then." She kicked off her sneakers and propped her feet on the coffee table. "And you probably never will."

"Will never do what?" Josh asked, walking into the room.

"Cut her hair."

"Don't. It looks sort of romantic," Josh said, tossing a handful of popcorn in his mouth. He put

55

the bowl on the table, shoving aside Amanda's feet.

"I'll cut it if I want to!" I said, surprised at how sharp I sounded.

Josh rolled his eyes.

Amanda broke in. "Don't worry, Josh. Naomi won't cut it. She hates changes."

"Glad to hear that," Josh said, grinning. He pulled me down on the couch beside him. Carefully he pushed my hair out of my face and pecked my cheek. He dug his other hand into the popcorn bowl.

"I might surprise you one of these days," I said, wriggling away from Josh and getting up from the couch. I was sick of everyone thinking I was so predictable. "Maybe I'll shave it all off!" I threatened as I began braiding my hair.

Amanda made a hooting sound.

Max cracked up.

Josh flicked at the TV remote. "Nah, that's not your style," he said, sounding very sure of himself.

My stomach was churning as I fumbled in my pocket for my barrette. After Dylan, I didn't want anyone else to touch my hair.

I sat on the rug and began putting Sharon Jane's blocks in her toy box. I was thinking what an awful person I must be. I had known these people forever. And at the moment, I felt as if they were three perfect strangers. They actually thought they knew me, but they had no idea what was going on in my life, or in my heart.

Looking at Josh, I suddenly felt a stab of guilt. I knew I wasn't in love with him. He wasn't a very romantic person, but we liked each other. We were sort of going together. I wondered what "sort of" meant to Josh. I wondered what it meant to me. I wondered what Dylan was doing just then. . . .

I wondered why every other thought that crossed my mind had to do with Dylan.

What was wrong with me? I was supposed to be on the couch cuddling Josh. Instead, I was safely across the room, cuddling dreams of Dylan.

"Naomi," Josh said.

I jumped.

"You look really different tonight. . . . You look . . ." He paused to search for the word.

Guilty, I said silently.

"Happy."

"Happy?" I repeated, staring right at him.

"What's different about that?" Max asked, unzipping his sweater.

Amanda narrowed her eyes to study me. "I think Naomi's falling in love with acting."

I closed Sharon Jane's toy box. "As usual," I said, trying to keep my voice even, "Amanda is right."

The boys zoned in on a TV show. Amanda zoned in on me. "So, you haven't mentioned Dylan tonight," she said, plunking herself down on the rug beside me. She thumbed through one of Sharon Jane's storybooks. I got the distinct feeling she was fishing for something.

"What's there to mention?" I tossed off. "We rehearsed the same old scenes for the play. Mainly I rehearsed with Dave Martin. Beauty's dad."

"I thought today might be the big day."

I had no idea what she was talking about.

Amanda leaned forward and tugged my braid. "Have you forgotten K-Day? Kiss Day?"

"As if you'd let me!" I retorted. I dug my toes into the thick-pile rug. Forget? All week long I had dreaded the moment when I'd have to kiss Dylan. Now that I had almost kissed him for real, I think I dreaded it more. I wasn't sure how I could pretend to kiss the Beast when, really, I was dying to have Dylan himself kiss me.

"I don't envy you that one."

"He's not bad looking, Amanda."

"Bad? No, he's handsome . . . if you like his type. I personally think he can't hold a candle to Josh in the looks department. But I just get the feeling he's shifty . . . dishonest. I don't know. Maybe all actors are like that."

"Like what?" I said, straightening up. I wasn't sure I wanted to hear what Amanda's theory of actors was.

"Like you never know who you're talking to."

Hadn't I been thinking the same thing myself that afternoon? Had Dylan really almost kissed me, or had I imagined it? Had he really been able to turn off his feelings so fast? I sure hadn't. Or had he had any real feelings at all to turn off?

"You know what I mean . . . about actors. Dylan's like that, isn't he? One minute a biker, and—"

"Amanda, did anyone ever tell you you talk too much?" I asked, jumping up. "Dylan's who he is. I'm not going to kiss him, anyway. I'm going to kiss the Beast. Remember? This is make-believe. A play. I'm having a great time rehearsing for this production. And I'm getting sick of you always trying to put my leading man down."

"You don't have to be so defensive," she countered.

"I'm not being defensive," I snapped. "I'm just getting tired of you acting as if you know everything."

"I know *you*, Naomi." She arched her eyebrows and stared at me.

"Maybe you don't," I mumbled as she flounced over to Max and deposited herself on his lap.

Chapter Five

"ONE WEEK AND three days. Can you believe we've only known each other just over a week?" Dylan's voice resonated through the Pizza Palace.

It was Friday, and he'd dragged me off school grounds for lunch. School rules stated that freshmen and sophomores couldn't leave the campus during school hours, and I had never eaten outside the lunchroom before. Dylan said it was time for me to learn to break some rules. It was time to celebrate. To celebrate a week of us. Of our new friendship.

"One week, three days, four hours, and twenty minutes," I told him. I wanted him to know I had been counting every wonderful minute. Still, a part of me was nervous that I'd get caught by some teacher here at Pizza Palace. I was terrified of detention.

Another part of me was thrilled that I was doing something just a little dangerous.

But most of me was just amazed how good it felt sitting across from Dylan.

Dylan's face flickered into a smile. "Good of you to keep track." He propped his elbows on the table and leaned toward me.

I took a deep breath and forced myself back in the seat. What in the world was happening to me?

"My life before the play was the pits," he told me.

"I don't believe that."

"Ah. A very perceptive person," he said, then leaned back to let the waiter put our pizza on the table. He handed me a slice and grabbed one for himself. "No, I just wanted to see if you cared."

I flicked a straw wrapper across the table at him.

He flicked it back and continued. "Life has not been the pits. I like Revere Hills. I even like living with my dad. But it's sure more fun living here now that I know you, going to school just to see you around."

"Before the play I never saw you anywhere." The thought still staggered me. Our school was huge, but how in the world could I possibly have missed someone like Dylan?

"Me too—I mean, I never saw you, either. I must have been blind." He tapped his straw like a blind man's cane across the table, and stabbed a slice of pepperoni off my pizza.

61

I slapped his straw away. He popped the pepperoni in his mouth and grinned at me.

I grinned back. Did I smile so much before I met Dylan?

"You live with your dad," I stated. "You mentioned that. . . ." I let the sentence hang in the air. I still didn't *really* know much about him. Except his passion for acting. And that his favorite pizza had extra cheese, meatballs, pepperoni, and sausage on top. Just like mine. Sometimes I wondered exactly who the real Dylan was. It was hard to tell when he was for real from when he was acting.

"Yeah, I live with my dad." Dylan nodded. He picked pieces of sausage off his slice of pizza and deposited them on mine. "I moved back here to be with him when my mother decided to get married again. I don't like the guy she's marrying." For once Dylan's voice sounded a little flat.

"It's not easy changing your whole life when you're a senior," I said, baiting him, hoping he'd go on and tell me about who he was before Masques, before coming to Revere Hills, before knowing me.

"No. It's not." He paused just long enough to tear off another slice of pizza. "And except for Masques, I don't have time for after-school activities. For just hanging out." He sounded wistful.

"Your job . . ."

"Yeah." He paused. "I work for my dad at his shop." He tapped his straw against his glass. "My dad's a repairman . . . a good one," he added, but he sounded a little defensive.

"I've heard."

He gave me a hard look.

"He owns the Double-R Repair and Fix-It Shop in Keaton Corners, doesn't he? I mean, that's where you live." I hurried to cover my blooper. I had never told Dylan that I had heard about him from my friends.

He relaxed. "That's the spot. The other side of town."

I finally understood why Dylan was being so defensive. He thought of himself as a person from the wrong side of the tracks. And then I realized Amanda probably did too, and Josh, and even Max. Our parents were doctors and lawyers, and Judge Munoz was running for governor next year.

Dylan's dad fixed their lawn mowers, snow-blowers, and blenders.

"Nope," I said lightly. "Different town entirely. You don't know your local geography yet." I stopped to slip on my jacket.

"I know enough about it." His tone was not light.

Then I did something I'd never done before. A week earlier—four days earlier—I would have pretended I didn't know what he was talking about just to spare his feelings. To avoid making a scene. But now, after a couple of no-holds-barred let-loose days of acting exercises and rehearsals with Dylan, I

63

wasn't the same old polite, let's-not-make-waves sort of person. I had become a girl who preferred to let her hair down.

"Look, Dylan Russo," I said as I lifted my hair over my coat and shouldered my backpack. "Wherever you live, I'm your friend. Keaton Corners is as good a place as any."

He stood up and looked me straight in the eye. "Now, how did I know you'd say that?"

I turned away quickly and looked up at the clock. Thoughts of Keaton Corners and Dylan vanished. "It's one o'clock. I'm going to be late for social studies!"

We raced each other across the parking lot into the front door. As we burst into the front hall, the second warning bell was ringing. "Oh, no! I'm in trouble now!" I wailed.

"I'm in trouble now!" he wailed back, mocking me.

I glared at him and bolted for my locker. All my books for afternoon classes were inside. This was no time for jokes or theater games.

He followed behind me. I had a feeling he was imitating the way I walked.

"Aren't you late for something too?" I asked. He leaned against the locker next to mine and looked on with interest. I flubbed the combination twice. When I finally got the lock opened, the locker wouldn't budge. Dylan gently shoved me aside and gave it a light kick. The door miraculously popped open.

He planted himself in front of it and wouldn't let me hang my coat up or get my books. "I've got study hall," he informed me calmly. "A free period. Time to memorize, à la Mrs. Bothwraithe. We have our big scenes coming up this afternoon, you know."

I caught my breath. "Right. Today. I forgot." I really had forgotten. Though at that second, with Dylan's face inches from my nose, I couldn't imagine how I had.

Today was K-Day. Kiss Day.

The final warning bell blared. "I've got to run," I told him. But I just stood there, unable to move.

"I've noticed," he said, smiling. And I got a crazy feeling that he was trying not to laugh at me.

"I'm going to be *very* late for social studies. I'll get detention."

"Sounds like a good experience. I mean, actors should always be looking for new experiences."

"Stop it, Dylan!" I cried. He was still blocking my locker.

"I bet you get straight *A*'s in social studies."

I rolled my eyes. "So?"

"How about another new experience—"

"Like what?" I tried to jockey around him. He wouldn't budge.

"What's the craziest thing you've ever dreamed of doing?" He didn't give me enough time to blush. "I mean *legal* fun." He paused for just a beat. "Something no one thinks you'd ever dare to do."

I thought for all of one second. "Cut my hair!" I

blurted, then clapped my hand over my mouth. How could I say that to Dylan, who had made me love my long hair more than ever?

"Great!" He punched his fist into the palm of his hand. "All right. Let's do it—now!"

I was speechless.

"You know that place in the mini-mall behind the school?"

"Shear Madness?" I felt like I was on some kind of roller-coaster ride in high gear.

"Right. My stepmom goes there. They do haircuts in half an hour for ten bucks—you'll only cut one class," he added wickedly. "Just think what people will say when they see you!"

I knew I should say no. But then again, why shouldn't I do it? I bit my lip. "Cut class to get a haircut!" I said in surprise. Suddenly I remembered Amanda. *She'll never cut it!* The expression on her face when she came over tonight for our weekly workout session would be worth it.

"Yeah, cut class." He mocked my horrified tone. Then he tousled my hair and moved away from my open locker. His tone softened and he sounded almost wistful. "It's a beautiful day, and—"

"I've never cut a class in my life."

"Always a first time. . . ."

"Well—what if we get caught?"

"Trust me. We won't. We'll cut across the back parking lot, past the crew house down by the river. The river path leads right to the Plymouth mini-mall.

66

We can rehearse our lines while we're waiting for them to take you." He reached for my hand.

I hesitated only a second. Then I took his hand and held it tight and felt like I was about to set out on the adventure of my life.

"Hey, why don't you cut your next class, too!" Dylan suggested forty minutes later, as we slipped back into the hallway. "You need at least another hour to get used to the brand-new you!" Dylan was laughing, but he couldn't take his eyes off my face. He adored my haircut.

So did I. Especially after he told me it made me look "all eyes."

I'll admit I *was* more than a little tempted. I couldn't imagine leaving Dylan and heading for French. My haircut had taken only twenty minutes, and the rest of the time we hung out by the river, rehearsing our lines. I still felt connected to Dylan, to the Beast. Actually, I wasn't sure which right then.

"Not that I'm trying to get you to do something you'll regret . . ." A smile played around Dylan's lips.

I shook my head no. Reality called. I reined in my daydreams of spending every afternoon of my life with Dylan, and sighed. "It was fun. But don't tempt me. Please."

"Just asking," Dylan said, not quite able to take his eyes off me.

The way he was staring at me made me blush.

For a moment I felt as if we were back in the scene we had just finished rehearsing. The scene when Beauty first starts to realize the Beast is not such a terrible creature, but deserving of her pity.

"I can't. I better not be late, either. Monsieur Manet doesn't even like us to miss class when we're dying of the flu or something."

"Okay," he said, as he backed off in the opposite direction. "Let's have lunch again sometime."

"Right . . . but I'm not sure I want to try my luck wandering off school grounds like that again."

"Or cutting class."

We were a good two yards away from each other, and French was still miles away. Almost no one else was left in the halls.

"See ya later," he called out. His words echoed through the locker-lined hallway.

"Later! At the theater." My heart lifted. Forty-five minutes from now. I continued to stare at him.

Dylan didn't budge.

I turned first and broke into a full run, almost knocking down Mr. Wernet, the hallway monitor.

"Naomi Peters?" He stared at me as if not quite able to place me. Inwardly I cheered. I looked *that* different. "Are you late?" he asked, sounding shocked.

"Just a little," I told him. He probably would have had a heart attack if he'd caught me cutting class last period and found me with Dylan. I was still pale at the thought when I skidded into French class.

Everyone was at their desks.

"*Bonjour*, Mademoiselle Peters," said Monsieur Manet. "You are today a bit late, *un peu tard, non?* New haircut?" he added with lifted eyebrows. *"Tres chic!"*

"Uh, yes . . . I mean, *oui*, I mean, *merci*." I dropped down into my front-row seat, right next to Josh.

I looked at him. He stared back at me, gaping at my hair. I could tell he didn't adore my new look. Then he stared at my hand. I was still holding a copy of the playbook. Dylan's copy, actually. His name was printed boldly on the cover and the spine, clear as day. The green-and-red border of a Pizza Palace napkin poked out from the page I had put in to mark the scene Dylan and I had been rehearsing.

Monsieur Manet cleared his throat. "*Maintenant*, now, since Mademoiselle Peters is *un peu tard*, a little late, I will have to repeat the assignment. Mademoiselle, we are having *un petit conversation*. You are to act like you're in a restaurant. One of you will be the waiter, the other will be the customer. You have a partner, Monsieur Davidson, *oui?*"

"Uh, yes . . . *oui* . . . Josh." I slipped the playbook into my bag and opened my French textbook. My hands were shaky, and the words on the page wouldn't come into focus. The napkin was a dead giveaway. Josh probably realized I'd gone for pizza. The playbook made it all too clear exactly *who* I'd

69

been with during lunch and after. I suddenly felt sneaky. It was a horrible feeling.

Josh slipped me a note. I opened it.

I was at the cafeteria.
WHERE WERE YOU?!!!!!!!
And . . . WHAT HAPPENED TO YOUR HAIR??????????

Seven exclamation points. I counted them twice to make sure. Not meeting the crowd in the cafeteria for lunch did not justify seven exclamation points. And ten question marks was an insult I was not going to tolerate.

I couldn't believe Josh was so freaked out. I looked up at him.

But Josh avoided my eyes. He shook his head with disgust and turned his seat to face me.

"We have exactly fifteen minutes to practice; then we have to present this dumb dialogue to the class," Josh informed me through tight lips.

Everyone else had paired up and begun murmuring and practicing their dialogues.

"Bonjour, mademoiselle," Josh began in a soft but sharp voice.

"You're the waiter?"

"Oui, je suis votre garçon ce soir."

He may have been telling me he was the waiter, but he sounded like he was ready to strangle me.

"Josh," I muttered, "I don't know why you're so mad at me."

70

"Parlez-vous seulement français, Mademoiselle Naomi!" the teacher interrupted, reminding us to speak only in French. He was strolling around the room, listening in on the various conversations.

"Oui, monsieur." I pretended to look in my dictionary, until he was out of earshot.

"I'm not so mad. I'm just really freaked. Where have you been?" Josh demanded. "You look really weird. What made you cut your hair?" He sounded personally insulted, as if I'd cut *his* hair off or something.

Before I could even think of an answer to that, Josh went on. "You weren't in social studies. Amanda detoured on her way to biology lab to tell me you hadn't turned up there, either."

"Either?"

"You weren't at lunch."

"Just not in the cafeteria, that's all."

"I can't believe you're acting this way."

"What way?" I challenged.

We were having our first real argument. And everyone was beginning to notice.

Jessica Bartoli and Ann Brunswick looked up from their dialogue and gaped at us.

"Mind your own business," I snapped. They turned away, and I stuck my tongue out at their backs.

Josh looked horrified.

"All I did was go out for pizza for lunch." I crunched the note I still held in my right hand.

"You went off campus for lunch," he said,

pushing his chair back from me, as if going off campus was contagious. "Sophomores do not do that!"

"What's the big deal?"

"It's against the rules, Naomi. I didn't think you were the sort of person to go around breaking rules. And you cut social studies, didn't you? Just to work on that play with Dylan—right? This whole theater thing is getting too much. You're acting like some starry-eyed airhead."

"I'm not an airhead, Josh Davidson. And I'm not going to die if I miss one social-studies class. It's not such a big deal. And besides, I'm not any *sort* of person at all," I said. "I'm just me. I wanted pizza for lunch and to work on the play a little more, that's all." I did not add that I had cut class to get my hair cut. Josh wasn't ready to hear about that.

"But I was waiting for you." Suddenly he sounded a little lost.

I racked my brain, trying to remember. "Did we have a date set up? Were we supposed to meet in the cafeteria?"

"Supposed to?"

I nodded, then spied Monsieur Manet making his way toward us. *"J'ai faim!"* I switched back to the dialog. *"Je voudrais des pizza!"* I added the pizza part just to get Josh. He turned red.

Monsieur smiled with pleasure as he passed.

"No, we weren't *supposed* to, but we always have lunch together." He looked down at me. His expression flowed from pained to confused to annoyed. "Everyone wondered what had happened to you. Amanda almost went to the school nurse when you weren't in social studies."

"Gimme a break!"

Josh set his jaw. "That's not fair. Amanda was worried."

"There's nothing to worry about. I just felt like doing something different for once."

Josh heaved a sigh and smoothed back his hair. He looked up at the ceiling, down at the floor, everywhere but my eyes. "I just thought we always had lunch together."

"Not always, Josh. It's just usually worked out that way. But now with the play, I might have to rehearse at lunch. Like today." I hadn't rehearsed a thing at lunch. I'd just had fun being with Dylan. But I had rehearsed afterward—we both had, very hard. Still, it was a half-truth and I felt a little uncomfortable. "Don't take it for granted I'll be there. Okay?"

Josh finally looked at me. He bit his lip. "Sure. I mean, what can I do about your rehearsals and all? It's got to be okay. I just don't want to lose track of you." He flashed a tentative smile.

I smiled back and touched his sleeve. I suddenly felt very sad. I didn't know what to say. We both knew he was losing me.

Chapter Six

"STAGE KISSES ARE always awkward. Even when you're an old pro at them," Judi Bender told Dylan and me that afternoon. She had cleared the theater of the other actors. Only Marnie and the construction crew were hammering away behind the backdrop. "So let's air our feelings now and get everything out in the open."

Our feelings? I knew Dylan must have been feeling something, because he was standing very stiff and straight on one side of a big papier-mâché rosebush. His arms were folded across his chest, and he'd avoided my eyes for the last ten minutes.

My feelings—I wasn't sure I was ready to hang them out for the world to see. Since I'd argued with Josh, my life had become one mass of mixed-up feelings. Mostly bad ones.

He'd said something about me becoming a different person. And he was right. Before today I never felt sneaky or dishonest. I wasn't sure I liked the person I was becoming.

Kissing Dylan had become something I didn't even know how to think about.

And what about Judi? What feelings could she possibly have? I looked at her now. She was focused on the back of the theater, watching the last cast members straggle out. She hadn't made a big deal of it, but I realized she had carefully orchestrated this rehearsal. Working the biggest group scenes first, then scenes with my father and me and the evil count who wanted to marry me. Until the cast had shrunk down to just two people.

The scene where the Beast is dying and Beauty rushes to save him was all that was left.

When the theater was empty, Judi turned back to us. "Okay. First of all, stage kisses are pretty technical things. You have to basically fake it. You use body language to make the audience think lots of hot and heavy stuff is happening."

I fanned my face with my script. I felt hot, all right. Dylan kept shifting his weight from his right foot to his left. We both caught Judi's eye, and all at once we were laughing. All three of us.

"Like I said, it's better to get it out in the open. But talking about stage kisses isn't the problem. Doing them is. First you need to get into character. Beauty," she addressed me as she always does in the middle of a scene.

Judi shooed me into the wing and then cued me for my entrance. I had to run around the back of the shallow set, up on a little platform, then down again to give the impression of rushing through space and up and down stairs into the Beast's garden. I held up the hoop of the practice skirt Dana had rigged for me, and half stumbled and tripped my way to Dylan's side. I kept waiting for Judi to stop me, to make me start the scene again.

I was definitely not in character.

I dropped not very gracefully beside Dylan, hard enough so my knees hurt. I barely stifled an "Ouch." He at least had the sense to have his eyes closed, though his heart was pounding so hard I could practically see it through his sweatshirt.

I was all nerves as I leaned over Dylan, picked up his head, and cradled him in my lap like I was supposed to. I felt him take a deep breath, trying to relax, to ease the tension. I leaned forward and pecked him on the cheek.

"That is not the kind of kiss I had in mind, Naomi."

I looked up. Judi was trying to smother a smile.

"Shall I go out and start again?"

She ignored the hopeful note in my voice. "No. Not necessary. Just try the kiss part."

This time I was able to picture myself saving the Beast's life. I kissed his cheek. Then I pecked him on the lips. His mouth was cold and he didn't respond to me. Suddenly I got really scared. I kissed him again. This time he kissed me back. A fifth-grade boy-kisses-girl-on-the-mouth-for-first-time sort of kiss.

It was awful. But he continued the scene. The Beast took my hand, and I pretended to pull him up. We were face-to-face. He wrapped his arms around me, drew me closer. First our noses, then our foreheads bumped.

"Ow!" he wailed, hopping back as if I'd hit him head-on with the force of a semi.

"Ow to you, too!" I cried, rubbing my forehead.

Our lips hadn't even gotten within kissing distance.

Judi laughed out loud. "Like I said, it gets awkward." She shoved us closer together. "It's good you're close in height. That makes everything easier."

"More dangerous, you mean," Dylan joked.

"Dylan," Judi instructed, "you lean so your head blocks her face from the audience. Naomi, you wrap your arms around him. Now, as you draw closer"—she made us draw closer—"you part your lips slightly so the audience thinks you're really going to get passionate. But your lips don't even have to really touch, if you don't want them to. The audience will fill the rest in."

We obediently followed Judi's instructions, step by step. Dylan put his arm around me so my face was slightly hidden. We parted lips, and then our faces touched. He turned me around so his back was toward the audience, and his face shielded mine from view.

And then he kissed me. It was more a messy peck on the cheek. It felt very silly. We broke apart, giggling, but the tension was all gone.

I admit I was a little disappointed.

Thankfully, Judi ended the rehearsal there. After we changed our clothes, I met Dylan on the stage, swinging his backpack by one shoulder strap. I felt light, and all my messy moods of before had lifted. I no longer worried about Josh and how upset he was. And I didn't have to worry about kissing Dylan on stage anymore.

"That wasn't too bad," I said as I followed Dylan down a couple of steps and into the side aisle of the theater.

"Thanks a lot." Dylan thumped his heart with his hand. "A guy gets wounded being rated 'not too bad.'"

I hit him with my notebook. "I mean, stage kisses aren't as hard as I thought they'd be." I couldn't believe how easy it was to say that.

"I don't think we've perfected them yet," he said. We strode together past Judi, who was sitting in a seat with her clipboard propped on her knees, making notes. "But it would help if we could both really get into character."

"It's tough beginning a scene right in the middle of the action and becoming Beauty or imagining you're the Beast," I told him. Then I remembered. "That book. The one about creating a character. You said you'd lend it to me."

Dylan stopped in his tracks. "I forgot all about it. You really should check it out."

"Bring it to the next rehearsal. Monday afternoon."

Dylan nodded, then slapped his forehead. "Why waste the weekend?" He checked his watch. "I work the night shift tonight. I don't have to be there until five thirty or so. Why don't I drive you home from school, and on the way we can stop at my place? I can get you the book then."

Before I could answer yes or no . . . before I connected the ride home with Dylan's motorcycle, Judi looked up from her clipboard. "We never did finish talking about playing that scene," she said in a very casual way.

"We didn't?" Dylan said, giving me a puzzled look. We backed down the aisle a few steps and leaned against the wall across from Judi.

"Like everything else," she said easily, "practice makes perfect, and that goes for stage kisses. But actors often get into trouble when they forget stage romances are just that—something that happens between two *characters* on stage."

Had Judi seen something between me and Dylan? What was she talking about?

Dylan surprised me. He straightened up and looked right at Judi. "You mean because we're thrown together so much, people—actors—start thinking they're more than just friends?"

Judi chuckled. "You could say that. But not much *thinking* seems to come into it. You share a very special relationship when you work together in the theater. You see parts of a person you think are bits of their soul, when really they're bits of their craft."

I must have looked really lost now. Judi reached out and playfully tugged at my sleeve. "Don't look so serious, Naomi. I'm just giving a high-school drama coach's word of warning. You seem like a pretty sensible person. Nothing's wrong with becoming *friends*."

I wanted to ignore the very slight emphasis she put on the word *friends*. I couldn't, though. She was afraid Dylan and I were becoming involved with each other.

"Not to worry," I said brightly to Judi. "Nothing to worry about on the just-friends front here."

"Great. See you Monday," she said. "And try to make it to the costume call tomorrow afternoon, Naomi. It won't take long."

"It better not," I murmured as Dylan and I headed out of the theater, into the school hall. "I'm really backed up on homework."

"Do you still want to pick up the book from my house?" he asked.

"Oh, right! Um . . . I'd like to," I admitted slowly. "But I've never ridden on a motorcycle before."

Dylan's eyes sparkled. "Then you're in for a treat."

"I don't know about that. . . . I mean, my—"

Dylan didn't even let me finish about how my

dad would kill me if the motorcycle didn't kill me first. "I know. You're probably scared. Everyone is the first time. Even *moi*! My dad taught me how to ride. He belongs to a bike club."

Visions of the grungy bikers parked outside Pulito's danced through my head.

Dylan must have read my mind. "Not the kind of club you're thinking. Mr. Cates from the bank is the president of this club." He laughed at my expression.

"You're kidding."

He shook his head and opened the door. A blast of cool wind greeted us. The sky was bright blue and the sun was still shining, though it was low in the sky. It certainly felt like November again.

"Isn't it cold for a bike?"

"Don't sound so hopeful. I won't let you off that easily. Just zip up your jacket. I've got an extra scarf and helmet, of course." We walked up to his Harley. I was glad he had a big bike. "I don't live that far. And I know a back road to where you live—Old Town Road, right?"

I nodded. "I don't think I'm going to like this," I said as he showed me how to fasten the helmet. He told me briefly how to lean with him into the curves and how he wouldn't drive too fast.

"You can trust me," he said.

As scared as I was, I suddenly wanted to try something else new. Just to see what it felt like.

I had tried acting, and so far that was a wonderful

new experience. I had cut a class and gone off campus for lunch and hadn't shriveled like the Wicked Witch of the West. Maybe I was born to ride motorcycles and just didn't know it yet.

Dylan gunned the engine a couple of times and swerved into rush-hour traffic. I closed my eyes and felt a scream work its way up my throat. But I was so intent on hanging on to Dylan and bracing myself against the noise and the wind, my voice died out.

The first five minutes were awful. The roar of the engine, the feeling of nothing between me and the road. I clung to Dylan as if he were a life jacket in the storm of late-afternoon traffic. But as soon as we turned off South Main and onto one of the smaller streets leading toward his part of town, I began to enjoy the ride.

"I like this," I tried to tell him. But I don't think he could hear me through his helmet, and the cold wind made it hard to talk. *This might be my first time on a motorcycle,* I thought, *but it's definitely not my last.* As we soared around the corner, and the red-and-white sign for his dad's fix-it shop came into sight, I was loving every minute of the ride.

If only Amanda could see me now! First she'd faint dead away. Then she'd get up and hit the phone wires and tell everyone we knew, starting with Josh, that Naomi Peters had really lost it.

I savored being a bad girl as Dylan pulled into the gravel parking lot. Then I threw my head back into the wind and laughed. I wasn't doing anything bad or wrong. I was just having fun, trying new things. Trying to find the real Naomi Peters.

Chapter Seven

"TELL ME YOU liked it!" Dylan said, as we both hopped off the bike at his dad's fix-it shop. He flung his arms open to the sky. "Isn't it a great feeling? The wind in your face, the road whizzing up at you. The freedom."

"I liked it. I liked it."

He laughed. I took off my helmet and touched my cheeks. They felt hot and windburned. I shook my hair, still surprised at how light my head felt now that my hair was so short. Above our heads the red-and-white repair-shop sign creaked on its hinges, and I decided I liked this place.

Dylan wheeled the Harley past a shed with an EQUIPMENT FOR RENT sign and parked his bike next to a small tractor. I looked around for his dad's house.

The shop was on a corner lot. The air smelled

faintly of paint and solvents and old rubber. A small two-story detached building housed the shop, and tall oak trees lined the back of the lot. Through the dried brown leaves I saw a modest-sized white clapboard house. The porch roof sagged a little, but it was exactly the way I had pictured it.

Dylan rounded the side of the shop. The back door was ajar, and shelves of old appliances and junk were visible through the cracked windows. As he walked, he whistled the theme song from the Disney movie version of *Beauty and the Beast*. There was a spring in his step, and his eyes were bright. He looked from the trees to the equipment shed to a ragged clump of frostbitten chrysanthemums. When he met my glance, his smile brightened. "So this is it. This is where I live."

I nodded and headed for the worn path between the trees that led to the side of the house.

"Wrong way!" He put his hands on my shoulders and steered me toward the shop. "It'll just take a minute to get the book."

"You live above the shop?" I was astonished. I looked up and noticed the red-checked café curtains over the second-floor windows. For a crazy moment I thought his whole family lived squashed together above the store.

"Sure thing. My dad has a whole other family with Millie, his wife—I have two half brothers and a half sister. The house is small, so when I moved here in August, they decided I was old enough to camp out on my own. I hang out at the house a lot—but this place is my own. Not much to brag about, but I like it." As he talked, he unlocked a door on the side of the building. A narrow flight of wooden steps led up to the second floor. "I've lucked out, I guess," he said, looking down at me from the third step. "I've got the best of both worlds. I have enough space to breathe and think and get away from the kids, but I don't have to be completely alone." He continued up the steps.

I stood riveted inside the door. I held it open and my mouth went very dry. What in the world was I doing? I'd never gone up to a guy's place alone. At Josh's or Max's we always just hung out in the kitchen or family room.

"Coming up?" Dylan looked down the stairs. His face was in darkness.

I suddenly felt ridiculous. Josh would surely think going up to Dylan's room was worse than eating lunch off campus or cutting class. And Amanda would just die, but she never had to know about this. And I was only there to borrow a book, after all.

"Sure," I answered, taking the stairs two at a time.

His place wasn't at all what I expected a boy's place to be. I had expected a mess—like Amanda's little brother's room, with clutter that engulfed the hall when you opened the door.

"It'll take a minute to find the book. I haven't looked at it myself since I unpacked."

He tossed his keys on the bed and dropped down on his knees in front of his bookshelf.

I looked around the room. A narrow bed was shoved against the wall right under the window. The window was open a crack, and a chilly breeze lifted the curtains. Yards and yards of books filled shelves made of planks stacked on concrete blocks.

There were no chairs, though there was one cushion on the floor in front of a nearly empty span of plywood resting on more blocks. Notebooks were stacked neatly beside a gooseneck lamp with a dented shade. There was no computer, just a fountain pen neatly capped beside a bottle of ink.

There was no VCR, no television, just a small CD/tape player on a milk crate.

It was the sort of place I always imagined living in. Not at all like my house, which had lots of stuff and not much space to think in.

"Make yourself at home," Dylan said.

I looked at his CDs. "You like jazz!"

"I love it. But only at night."

"I heard it playing in the background that time you called." I looked around the room and saw the phone on the desk. He hadn't called me from some cozy kitchen.

"You noticed?"

"I always notice stuff like that," I said, glad I was facing the bookshelf so he couldn't see me blush. I felt like a person who'd been eavesdropping.

"Poetry!" I said, excited. "I just love poetry." I scanned the spines of the thin books.

He was standing against the shelf, holding the Stanislavski book in his hand.

We just stared at each other a second. Dylan broke the silence first. "There's something about you, Naomi. You're full of surprises. Just when I think I know everything about you, I learn something new. I really like that."

I liked that in him, too. But I felt strange saying it.

Suddenly I realized I was alone in a guy's room and I was thinking about kissing him.

Dylan must have been thinking the same thing.

"Hey, we'd better get going." His voice came out sort of husky and weird. It might have been the fading sunlight slanting across the shelf, but his cheeks suddenly looked a little pink. The way mine felt.

Dylan handed me the Stanislavski book, and I made sure our hands didn't touch. I got up and headed for the door while Dylan grabbed the keys. Then I started down the stairs.

I heard the key turn in the door, and felt my cheeks grow cooler. It seemed safe to look back up at Dylan. Then something happened. My backpack shifted, and I almost lost my balance. I grabbed the banister but dropped the book.

We both bent down to pick it up off the step. This time our hands did touch. His flesh was warm and I could almost feel the blood racing in the veins beneath his skin.

I straightened up slowly. But he kept hold of my hand. His thumb was tracing little circles of fire against my palm. I had a feeling I should turn my head away. Run down the stairs. Hadn't Judi just warned us about this?

Dylan's head was even with mine, and our faces were suddenly very close. A part of me had waited my whole life for this moment. My knees had turned to mush. Dylan's lips were suddenly very close to mine, and before I closed my eyes I saw him smiling.

It wasn't a long kiss. It was sort of a brushing first kiss, but my heart soared. It wasn't my first kiss, after all. But it was the one that really mattered.

Then Dylan put his hands on the wall behind me and kissed me again. This kiss lasted longer than any kiss I'd ever had before. I drowned in it and couldn't have moved if I'd wanted to. I felt as if my heart were kissing his heart, my soul kissing his soul.

When I broke away, I felt heady—like a diver who'd come up too fast for air.

I reached out then and touched his earring with my finger.

He smiled his mysterious smile and looked right into my eyes. I felt as if he knew everything about me. *Everything. If I stand here one more minute,* I thought, *I will never have another secret. Nowhere private to go. No place to hide.*

I wrenched my eyes away from his, turned, and ran down the creaky stairs. I pushed open the door and burst outside.

The sun blazed over the brilliant white of the repair-shop sign, and my eyes were dazzled. It took a moment to adjust. I felt Dylan walk up behind me, but we didn't touch. I was suddenly afraid to look at him, to break the spell. He pocketed his house keys and led the way toward his bike.

We didn't hold hands. We just walked past the hulks of broken lawn mowers and generators and refrigerators to the spot next to the repair-shop truck, which had parked next to his bike while we were upstairs. He put his key in the bike ignition and handed me the extra helmet.

"So this guy . . . Josh . . ." was the first thing Dylan said. And I just swallowed hard.

I didn't want to talk ever again. I just wanted to keep kissing him, looking at him. But this *was* the real world, I had to remind myself, even though I thought I had stepped into a true romance at last.

"Is it serious? I mean, are you . . . ?" I heard the fear in his voice.

How can you ask that? I thought. I could still taste his kiss. My mouth couldn't even say the name Josh just then. But I cleared my throat and took a breath. "No. I mean, we are dating each other, but it's not serious. It's not exclusive. Nothing like that." *Nothing like what just happened!*

I wasn't lying about seeing other guys. Really, I wasn't. No one else had ever asked me out, but if they had, I wouldn't have let seeing Josh stop me. That kiss with Dylan just now had proven it. "He's just a friend. . . . Well, maybe a little more than that, but we sort of fell in together when everyone else in our crowd paired off."

He nodded. He understood.

I got behind him on the bike and wrapped my arms around his waist. I pressed my face into his back and wished I could melt away all the layers of his jacket, his sweater, his T-shirt that came between us. I wondered if his heart was still pounding as fast as mine.

Dylan revved up the engine. Before we pulled out, he reached back without turning around and touched my cheek. "Hey, a guy needs room to breathe," he said. "To drive one of these things," he added after the slightest pause.

I loosened my grip and sat back in the seat a bit, feeling my cheeks grow hot. Was Dylan upset with what had just happened? The kiss had felt so real, so deep, I couldn't bear any distance between us. Maybe kisses like that were everyday things to Dylan.

A man with a Double-R T-shirt came out of the shop. He gave Dylan and me a funny look as we pulled out of the lot. I tried to ignore it. I wondered if Dylan always had girls up in his room. The wind suddenly felt cold, right through my sweater and suede jacket, and the sun dipped down behind the church tower in a blaze of red.

If you take back streets, the trip from Keaton Corners to Old Town Road, where I live, is a short ride, but my mind must have traveled a million miles in the space of fifteen minutes. One minute I felt close to Dylan and was sure he had felt just as close to me. The next minute I wondered whether I was playing the fool.

What was Dylan feeling, anyway? I ached to ask him. Yet I was terrified of what the answer might be. Did he regret kissing me like that? Did he think maybe Judi was right, that getting involved with each other away from the set might be a bad idea?

The thought of Judi's little lecture made my heart stop. Stage romances—two people working closely together who get carried away—were par for the course. And our play *was* so romantic. I was pretty sure the guy I was falling in love with was Dylan. But had he just kissed Beauty and not Naomi?

My mind was still whirling as we turned the corner of Old Town Road. It's a sleepy street without much traffic, and my house sits on the far end. "I live there," I yelled to Dylan over the roar of the engine, pointing over his shoulder down the street.

Then a blur of orange fur bounded off the sidewalk after a bird.

"Pebbles!" I heard myself scream as the Harley hurtled toward my cat.

Dylan swerved, and the motorcycle tilted crazily as he avoided the cat. For a moment my whole life seemed to stop. Then somehow the bike straightened up. And with a last gun of the motor we half skidded into the loose gravel at the end of our driveway and stopped.

"That was close!" Dylan said. "That cat has gotta be down to eight lives now."

"*That cat* is Pebbles," I said, shakily getting off the bike. My legs were trembling and I could hardly undo my helmet. Dylan kicked down his brake, turned off the engine, and got off. He reached out and helped me with the helmet strap.

"Hey, don't be so shaken up. The cat is fine. Is it yours?"

I swallowed hard and tried to speak. I was still scared. We had almost killed Pebbles. And we had almost been killed trying to avoid her. Dylan's hand was so close to my mouth, it made my world turn a bit woozy.

"You're some driver," I finally managed to say, taking a step or two back. I handed him the helmet. "Pebbles doesn't run out into the street often, but every now and then . . . Dad says she's going to be squashed one of these days. We try our best to keep her in." I was babbling. "Thanks for missing her."

Out of the corner of my eye I could see my

father's Acura parked behind my mother's Volvo. They were both home. They'd probably heard me scream, the bike roar. They'd probably seen the whole thing. I gulped.

Dylan gave a casual shrug of his shoulders. "All in a good day's driving. See, I told you you could trust me."

"Um, yeah." I just stood there a second. "Thanks for the ride," I said. I brushed off my overalls and studied my boots.

He held my glance a moment, then reached out and ran his fingers through my hair. The gesture was so tender. I touched his hand; then I realized anyone could see us from the house. I dropped my hand and stepped back.

"I'd better get going."

"Wait."

I'd started to turn away. I stopped and faced him again.

"What happened back there?" His voice sounded a little tight.

"With the cat?" I pretended not to understand. I was still too scared to talk about us. I wasn't even sure there was an "us."

"Judi tried to warn us . . ."

I nodded.

His shoulders tensed up a bit. "About stage romances."

"Right. How—well—we'll be thrown together a lot, and the play is sort of romantic . . ."

"And maybe we should just be friends for a while." Dylan said it. I couldn't see his face in the twilight, but his voice had almost no expression. As if he were saying his lines badly.

"We hardly know each other," I added with a sinking heart.

Friends. I felt a surge of relief, a surge of dread. But "friends" was something I could handle. For now. Friends was real. Romance—that might be make-believe.

"Three weeks isn't very long to know someone," he added.

"I'd better go," I said again as I looked back to the kitchen. "I've got to help my mother with dinner, or I'd ask you in."

"Oh, no. No. But sometime, maybe." He backed away from me.

We stood there a moment just staring at each other.

"Friends," I repeated.

"Right . . . for now. Maybe take it slow. . . . I'll see you tomorrow."

"Rehearsal." I told myself this was sensible. Proceed with caution. Be careful, Naomi. Hadn't Judi said that to us?

"Till then."

We were still staring at each other.

"Naomi!" It was my father's voice. I could tell from the tone that he wasn't happy.

"Coming, Dad," I shouted back, and waved. He stood a moment with his hands on his hips, shaking his head. Then he went back inside and closed the door.

"You're not in trouble, are you?" Dylan sounded confused. His eyes were searching mine.

I felt if I stood there one more minute, we would kiss again—even though we'd just promised to be friends—right in front of the house, where everyone could see. My dad. The neighbors. Amanda, who lived two doors down.

"I'd better go." I wrenched my eyes away from Dylan's and ran down the driveway toward the side kitchen door.

I waited a moment on the side porch. I wanted my face to cool off, my heart to slow down before I went inside. I listened for the sound of Dylan's bike leaving, roaring off down the street. For the longest time I heard it idle. I realized he was listening for me to go inside, for the door to close.

"Naomi Peters, you get in here right now!"

I jumped at the sound of my father's voice. It was loud and angry this time, and I was scared. My father never raises his voice. He's normally a quiet, soft-spoken person.

"Naomi!"

"Coming, Dad!" I cried, and threw open the door. I slammed it shut. Then Dylan's bike roared off.

I kicked off my boots in the mudroom, and wondered what had just happened. Had I fallen in love? Was *this* romance? Had Dylan really meant it when he said we should cool down and just be friends?

Was this the beginning of a love story, or had it come to a sudden end in the space of fifteen minutes between Keaton Corners and Old Town Road?

I headed for the kitchen. My finger touched my lips where Dylan had kissed me, and I wondered how I could ever be just his friend.

Chapter Eight

BY THE TIME I got into the house, dinner had already been served, but my stomach was on overdrive. I was nauseous. I was in love. I was doomed. And I certainly wasn't ready to face my father.

Oh, Dad was back to his soft-spoken self. But don't let the soft part fool you. He had the look that meant he was about to make some awful rule.

After eating his soup in silence for several long moments, he said, "I'm of half a mind to ground you, Naomi."

"Ground me!" I shouted. "Because Dylan was nice enough to give me a lift home from rehearsal?"

"On a motorcycle!" my mother shrieked back, lifting her napkin to her mouth. "And what did you do to your hair?"

"More to the point, you know exactly how I feel about motorcycles—"

"Prejudice . . . pure prejudice," I shot back.

My father's anger was absolutely bulletproof. He went on without missing a beat. "He was driving recklessly, disturbing the whole neighborhood—and he almost killed Pebbles!"

"He did not. Pebbles almost killed herself." I reached down and patted the cat, who was sitting on my feet, hoping for a snack. "Dylan saved her. Anyone else probably would have hit her."

Dylan's act of heroism did not impress my dad. Far from it. "*You* almost got killed," he said.

My mother let out a small gasp and then touched my father's sleeve. "She is all right now, though."

"No thanks to that boy. And besides, he is *not* the sort of boy I'd picture you with. He looks like bad news to me."

I couldn't believe it. My father sounded like some throwback to the Middle Ages.

I decided to try a new approach. "Just because someone rides a Harley doesn't mean he's bad news. Mr. Cates at the bank rides one. And you wouldn't ground me for seeing him, would you?"

My father tried to digest this. He was still mad, but now he was the one trying not to laugh. "Mr. Cates has nothing to do with this. I care about who you date. I like Josh. I thought you were dating him. He's a sensible boy, and we've known him forever. He's the kind of boy you should be with, Naomi. Not with some troublemaker on a bike."

"I am not *dating* him," I blurted, hoping my face was red enough from yelling to camouflage my blush. "He's in the play with me, and he gave me a ride home. Dylan holds a job and goes to school full-time. And just because a guy gives you a ride home doesn't mean you're about to marry him!" I snapped, but for one wild, brief second, a wonderful image of me and Dylan on his bike, riding off into the sunset, flooded my mind.

An even wilder picture replaced it fast. My father would go ballistic if he ever found out about my going to Dylan's place alone . . . or about that kiss.

My twelve-year-old sister, Karen, gaped at all of us.

"Are we having a family fight? At the dinner table?" She sounded positively gleeful.

"Very observant," I answered as I shoved my plate away.

"Naomi, what's happening to you?" My mother finally pulled herself together and spoke in a more normal tone. She flicked a crumb off the tablecloth and stared at me. We have the same pale eyes that change color as our moods change. Right now her eyes were dark and worried. She also kept looking at my hair like it was glued on the head of a stranger. I couldn't tell if she loved it or hated it short. She just heaved a huge sigh and leaned back in her seat. "You've always been such an easy child—so even-tempered, so sweet. You've always had the nicest friends. Now you've

100

got this strange boy who calls you at all hours—"

"He called after eleven *once*!"

"And spoke a different language—'yo!' or 'ho!' "
My mother shook her head in disgust at the memory.

I cringed. If only Dylan hadn't said "Yo" to my
mother on the phone.

"Naomi, it worries me how much you've
changed recently," she said. "I don't even know you
anymore."

"Of course I'm changing!" I exclaimed. And I
instantly regretted saying it, because she looked so
hurt. But something in me charged on. "I'm fifteen.
You're the one who said when you're fifteen everything changes all at once." I balled my napkin in my
hand. I felt like throwing it at someone. Instead, I
hurled more words like darts at my mother. "I'm
being a normal fifteen-year-old girl!"

"She's beginning to get a life!" commented Karen.

"You're beginning to annoy me," I said, glaring
at Karen.

"Stay out of this, Karen," my father said.
Meekly she went back to her mashed potatoes.

Dad's tone shifted. "Naomi, is there something
you need to tell us?"

I couldn't believe it. I rode home once with a
boy on a motorcycle, and now my parents thought I
was in some kind of trouble. Drugs probably, or
who-knew-what teen dangers, lurked in the back
of their minds.

Karen leaned forward in her seat.

"Clear the table, Karen," my mother ordered. "And start loading the dishwasher."

"Do I have to?" she whined.

"Now."

Karen gritted her teeth and grabbed the salad bowl. "Just when you're getting to the good part," she grumbled as she passed my chair.

My father waited to continue until Karen was in the kitchen. "Your behavior is changing. You've been overreacting to everything lately. We're concerned about you." His voice was so calm and even, he sounded like he was reciting lines from a drug-counseling brochure. I couldn't stand it. In our house life is lived in a whisper. No one ever yells; everything is "discussed." Since Masques, since becoming Beauty, since Dylan, I had stopped whispering—I had begun to shout!

"You wouldn't understand," I retorted loudly. "But don't worry. Nothing's wrong with me, Dad. I'm not doing drugs, and I aced my midterms. Maybe it's just like Karen said. Trouble-free, quiet Naomi has finally gotten herself a life."

My parents looked helplessly at each other, then at me.

"Just don't lock us out of it," my mother said in an odd, sad voice.

I felt like I was going to cry. This was the first time in my life that I didn't feel I could talk to my parents. They obviously didn't understand anything I was going through.

I pushed back my chair from the table. "Look, I'm not hungry. I'm going upstairs," I whispered.

"We won't ground you this time," my father said before I left the room. "We understand about the play, rehearsals and all—" He cleared his throat. Just when I thought he was finished, he added, "But I never want to see you on a motorcycle with that boy—or anyone else—again!"

"Never see . . ." I turned on my heel to face him. He had said *see*. Then I met his eye and half smiled. "Okay, Dad. You'll never *see* me on a bike with Dylan or anyone else again." Behind my back I crossed my fingers as I said that.

At that point I usually would have barricaded myself in my room and burst into tears. Then I'd have phoned Amanda and we'd commiserate about parents and rules and the trials of love. But of course I couldn't call Amanda this time—she thought Dylan was bad news too.

Before I reached my room, the doorbell rang. My mother answered it. It was Josh.

"Naomi's upstairs," I heard her tell him. "Josh is here!" she called up the stairs. Mom managed an even tone, but I could tell she wouldn't cover for me if I said I didn't feel well or couldn't come down.

"Be right there." I went to the bathroom, threw water on my face, fluffed out my hair, and took a deep breath. Five minutes later I headed down the steps, without much enthusiasm.

Josh was waiting in the family room. "Hi," he

said, smiling. He was standing by the window.

"Hi," I said back, not sure what he was doing here. After our fight this afternoon, I didn't think Josh wanted to be within a mile of me. Suddenly he was in the past tense, as far as boyfriends went. I was miserable and embarrassed and confused. My mind was racing. I had to tell him I wanted to be just friends. But I couldn't do it. I wasn't ready to upset him like that.

"I know this is your workout night with Amanda."

I'd forgotten all about that. "She's not here yet."

Josh didn't seem surprised by that fact. "Right. I knew you'd be home, though, so I came over. Uh—I wanted to apologize."

I just shrugged. I wasn't sure he was the one who should be apologizing here.

"I like your hair. It's pretty," he blurted after an awkward pause.

"My hair?" I stared at him, then giggled. "Oh, thanks."

"So we're still friends?" he asked, an immense smile spreading across his face.

"Of course." No doubt about that. Josh was someone I could be friends with forever. Did he really think our argument was just about my hair? That I was willing to risk our friendship together because he didn't like the way it was cut? Our argument was about giving me space to grow and change.

Josh heaved a sigh of relief and plunked himself down on the family-room sofa. "I just got a little afraid this afternoon," he said, with more feeling than I wanted to hear. He'd angled himself into one corner of the sofa, and now expected me to sit next to him. I pressed back harder against the door and clasped my hands tight behind my back. I didn't want to spend the evening sitting on a sofa with Josh. I prayed that Amanda would turn up soon.

"Well," he continued, "I took a chance you'd forgive me, so I brought over a stack of movies. Video Fever was having their end-of-month dollar night."

I couldn't help but frown. "But Amanda should be here . . ."

"She can watch them too. She hates working out," Josh added with a chuckle. "C'mon—we haven't done this in a long time."

"Ages," I admitted. "I used to love dollar night." Until this fall Amanda, Max, Josh and I had always exploited dollar night with a vengeance, putting homework and everything else on hold.

"We don't have much time for fun anymore," he said, voicing my very thought. "Midterms, school—it's all getting crazy." He stacked his videos on an end table. "I was thinking of starting up a new Film Classics Club in school."

"What happened to Legal Eagles?"

"That too," he said. "But I kind of miss doing

stuff with you after school. I thought you'd be interested in a film club."

"Why?"

"Because of this theater bug you've caught."

"Right. But I don't have time for other clubs."

"When the play is over, I meant."

Just then the phone rang. I muttered a quick prayer of thanks to whatever god or goddess rules the phone lines and grabbed it on the second ring. This was definitely not the time for Josh to hear about my plans for a future in theater.

"Yo—Naomi?"

It was Dylan. I felt the blood drain from my face, then whoosh up again. "It's you!" I couldn't keep the joy from my voice. Then I remembered Josh. I peeked over at him and watched him study the back of a video box. "I can't talk right now."

"You're in some kind of trouble there, aren't you? Because of me." He sounded so worried.

"Not exactly. But sort of."

"The motorcycle?"

"Among other things," I replied carefully.

"I'll make it short, then."

I longed for him to make it forever, but I had to be careful of Josh. And what if my dad picked up the extension or something?

"I thought about us. About being friends. I—I think it's the right idea . . . don't you?"

I detected the smallest note of hope in his voice that maybe I'd say it was the worst idea anyone had ever had. I sighed. "It's all too much right now—*Dana*." I saw Josh look up out of the corner of my eye.

"You really *can't* talk now."

"Not at all."

"The phone's no good anyway. What about tomorrow night? Could we see each other then?"

How? I wailed inwardly. "Sure," I told him. I had a plan. "I'll see you at rehearsal."

"But I'm not at rehearsal." He sounded puzzled—but only for a second. "Oh, I get it. The motorcycle, your dad—you don't want me to pick you up at your house."

"You can't."

There was a funny silence. "Oh. Listen, Naomi, I don't like sneaking around."

"Please . . ."

"Okay. I'll meet you right after rehearsal in the side lot at school, near the theater. How's six o'clock? We'll go somewhere and talk."

"Yes. Yes, I'd like that." I kept my back turned from Josh for a second.

Then Dylan hung up.

I put on what I hoped was a gloomy face and turned to Josh after I'd hung up.

"Who was that?" Josh asked.

"Oh, Dana. About costumes. There's been another snafu with my costume. And then I have to rehearse some scenes with Dave Martin and Candy Lawrence—you know, the girl who's playing my selfish ugly sister." I faked a disgusted laugh. "She never knows her lines." Which was true. Candy was a slow study, though she was a pretty good actress. "I promised to help her memorize."

"When?" Josh frowned.

I hesitated ever so slightly. "Tomorrow afternoon, after play rehearsal."

Josh's face fell. He shoved his fists in his pockets. "But tomorrow we're all supposed to go to the opening of the new roller rink at the mall."

"Oh, Josh, I can't. Not this week. These rehearsals are sort of intense. When this play is over, things will get back to normal."

I admit I should have told him then. Told him my real feelings. Told him I just wanted to be friends. Life certainly would have been simpler if I had. I doubted I'd be spending any more Saturday nights with Josh in the future. But I just had no idea how to break it to him.

"Are you all right?" Josh's voice was full of concern.

I realized I had been standing with my hand still on the wall phone, staring into space. "Uh, yes—well, no," I lied. "I've got a headache."

Josh looked worried. "I guess this isn't a good night for videos."

I shook my head. "It's been a long day, and tomorrow I'll be busy with the play. And don't even ask about how much homework I've let pile up." I looked at my watch. "Amanda has probably copped out for tonight. I'll have to call her."

Josh nodded. "I had a feeling she wouldn't show."

Something in his voice made me look up. Josh, unlike Dylan, was not a good actor. He was trying to hide something and failing miserably. That's when I realized Josh hadn't just turned up here with some scheme to start watching videos on Fridays again. He'd turned up because Amanda had told him to come over and make up . . . that he'd better watch out or he'd lose me to someone like Dylan.

"You'd better go now," I said. It was all I trusted myself to say. At that moment my worry about Josh and how to tell him about Dylan quickly evaporated. I was getting tired of my so-called oldest friends—especially Amanda Zukowski—butting in where Dylan and I were concerned.

I showed Josh to the door, being careful to keep my distance so he couldn't kiss me good night.

As soon as he was gone, I marched back into the family room, determined to tell Amanda to keep her nose out of my life!

Chapter Nine

"FAVORITE ICE CREAM?" Dylan barked his question to me the next night.

"Cherry vanilla!" I replied, curling my feet under me on the worn brown upholstery of the movie-theater seat.

"Chocolate-chocolate chunk," Dylan confessed solemnly. He dug his fist into the popcorn bucket.

"Favorite movie?" I asked.

"*Rebel Without a Cause.*"

"So that's why we're here tonight."

Dylan propped his feet on the back of the seat in front of us and jammed some more popcorn into his mouth. "What's your favorite flick?"

"*Gone With the Wind.*"

"I don't know about this, Naomi Peters." Dylan's expression shifted from joy to horror. "We don't love the same movies. I'm not sure we can be friends."

"We can't?"

Then Dylan gingerly offered me a kernel of popcorn. I opened my mouth, and his pinkie grazed my lip as he tossed the kernel in. A shot of warmth blazed up from the soles of my feet right through the top of my head.

He must have felt it too, because he turned, faced front, and carefully left space between us. We continued our banter but kept our eyes on the blank screen. "I guess we just don't have enough in common," he said. His tone was neutral.

"We don't." I pretended to be morose, but inside my heart was singing. We could try to be friends for now, for a little while, but I knew it was going to be just as hard for him as it already was for me. He liked me as much as I liked him, I was sure of it. "Except," I added brightly. "Though it may not be my favorite, I certainly do like *Rebel Without a Cause.*"

"I guess we wouldn't be here if you didn't like it," Dylan said comfortably.

I shifted in my seat slightly. I didn't feel quite as comfortable as he seemed to be. The real reason we were at the Keaton Corners Revival Theater was that it's miles from the Revere Hills mall, where Amanda, Josh, and Max were Rollerblading tonight. That's why I'd suggested going to a classic movie here. Thank goodness Dylan loves James Dean.

The houselights dimmed and the trailers came on. Groups of kids straggled down the aisles to the only seats left, all the way up front. We were in the very back row, my favorite place to sit.

The credits scrolled and the movie started. Our fingers touched when we both reached into the popcorn bucket at the same time. We held hands for a good ten minutes before Dylan leaned over. His breath tickled my ear as he said, "Are we still being friends?"

Something in his voice made me turn to face him. Our lips were so close. "Judi isn't going to like this," I whispered.

Dylan's eyes were shining in the dark theater light. "She did say practice makes perfect."

And by twenty minutes into the movie, our kissing was close to perfect.

I'd seen the movie at least ten times before that night, maybe even twenty, but I knew I'd never see it again without thinking of Dylan—the nubby feel of his sweater, the way his skin was soft on the back of his neck, the way his single earring felt cool and mysterious every time I touched it in the dark.

We were still kissing when the houselights came up. Dylan was the first to pull away, his cheeks flushed. He smoothed my hair and held me back at arm's length. "You're beautiful."

"And you're a beast!" I laughed.

He laughed too, as he reached across to help me put my jacket on.

As I glanced up toward the front of the theater, I saw the shock of my life—Amanda. I instantly went from hot to freezing cold. She was standing up, still facing the screen, scrambling into her new fake-fur coat. The red hair was unmistakable. So was the tall guy standing next to her—Josh. I couldn't see Max through the crowd, but I was sure he was there too.

"Let's get out of here. I'm feeling sort of hot." I didn't wait for Dylan to answer. I quickly scrambled over the couple next to us and out into the lobby. The Keaton Corners theater is pretty small, and there weren't many places to hide. Not many nooks or crannies.

"What's wrong?" Dylan came running up behind me. He handed me my scarf. I'd probably lost my gloves, but I didn't care. I wasn't going to go back to find them.

I looked past his shoulder. The crowd was thick, and it moved slowly out the theater doors. "Let's get out of here."

"Your parents?" He sounded horrified. "They're here."

"Parents? No. I'll explain later. Let's just leave. Now!"

Dylan had borrowed one of the repair-shop trucks that night. The cold temperature was one reason. I was sure the other reason was my dad.

When Dylan started toward Jonesy's, I quickly steered us in the direction of McDonald's, knowing that Amanda hated fast food. The nearest McDonald's was five miles away—ten miles from Jonesy's. We'd be safe there.

Fifteen minutes later we were sitting under bright fluorescent lights, a cardboard cutout of Ronald McDonald swaying over us. Not my idea of a romantic first date.

But romance wasn't exactly on my mind right then.

As I played with my burger, I told Dylan that I'd seen Amanda at the movie theater. But he didn't seem to understand.

"I don't get it. First your father doesn't want you to see me. Now your friends." He raked back his hair—seeming angry and hurt. "I thought I got the lead in the play because I was good. Now I think I was typecast. Dylan Russo—the Beast."

"Stop it, Dylan. Stop it." I looked at him. "You're being melodramatic. It's not like that. No one thinks you're a beast."

"Oh, boy, now I feel better," he said sarcastically. "Of course, it's a small point, considering that no one even knows me—" He stopped, and his voice shifted from anger to wonder. "Not even you."

"How can you say that?" I cried. I couldn't sit across from him anymore and watch the hurt in his eyes. I got up and sat beside him at the table, took his head in my hands and kissed him, right there in McDonald's. Someone behind us murmured something. Someone else giggled. But I didn't care. I just didn't care.

When we separated, Dylan's lips twitched into a soft smile. "Practice *does* make perfect."

He leaned back in his seat and offered me some of his soda. "I don't think what's happening between us happens often."

"I wouldn't know." I looked down at the table. "I've never had anything happen like this before. It's—it was different with Josh."

"Josh was there too, not just Amanda."

I nodded, wondering if love was worth losing all my oldest and best friends.

"I've never felt this way about anyone," Dylan quietly admitted. He tilted my chin up.

All he had to do was touch me and I turned to jelly. Is this what love feels like? Is this what I've been waiting all my life for?

Something inside of me shouted *Yes!*

Then I realized Dylan had been trying to tell me something. I forced myself to focus on his voice, not his lips.

"I've never felt this way with other girls I've dated." He shook his hair out of his eyes. "I just don't like all this sneaking around."

"We haven't been sneaking around . . . much," I countered.

Dylan gave a small laugh. "Naomi, we've only been out on one real date. Actually, we're still on it. But you don't want me to meet your friends. And your family doesn't want me to see you. I like you too much to sneak around. I won't do it."

"You're making this such a big deal," I said.

"So what are we going to do about it?"

My heart went cold. "Do?"

"Don't you get it, Naomi? I don't want to embarrass you in front of your family and friends. So if that's the way you feel, then let's just part company now . . . before it's too late. I like you too much to—" His voice broke off. He propped his forehead in his hands and muttered at the table. "To get more involved and then have to break it off."

"Break this off?"

He looked up and shook his head. "Don't look at me like that. Please," he begged, touching my lip with his finger.

I pulled back and nodded slowly. "You're right. I don't like hiding things from people. It's too complicated. I'll talk to Josh. But Dylan, can you give me a little time? I can't just blurt it out to him. I tried to last night, but I didn't know how. He's an old friend, and he'll be hurt. I promise I'll do it. I have to be fair to all of us."

Dylan smiled his beautiful smile.

I smiled back.

We celebrated my decision with a kiss.

"And your parents," he murmured.

"Ah . . . *that* . . ."

"One step at a time," he said, his voice full of sympathy. "Maybe they'll come around."

I couldn't picture that happening—ever. Then Dylan took me in his arms and all other thoughts left my head.

Chapter Ten

SUNDAY MORNING I stayed in bed, counting the hours until I'd see Dylan again. Monday was just too far away. Besides, if I lounged around the house, I wouldn't risk seeing Amanda.

I was pretty sure she hadn't spotted me with Dylan the night before, but I couldn't be positive. And I didn't want a showdown with her now. That would quickly spoil the wonderful memory of my first date with Dylan. I couldn't stand to hear one more of her predictions of broken hearts and ruined lives, or how I had turned into a flaky, stage-struck ditz.

Sometimes I think she's the one who should have gone into drama. She may not love romance, but she adored tragedy.

I ran my fingers through my hair and practiced looking wide-eyed and innocent in the mirror. I just had to see Dylan today. I decided to sneak out and visit him at work, so I'd need my acting skills more than ever. Though fooling Mom was barely a challenge anymore.

I waited till after lunch, when Dad and Karen had left to visit my grandparents, before I ventured out of my room. I packed up my library books and went downstairs. I poked my head into the study and saw Mom working on some accounts she'd brought home. She looked up over her glasses when I walked in.

"I'm going to bike over to the library," I told her. "My books are overdue."

"Isn't it cold to ride to the library?" She looked at her watch. "I can give you a lift and pick up some groceries at the convenience store on the way back." She began taking off her glasses.

"Don't be silly, Mom." I zipped up my parka. I hoped she hadn't noticed I was wearing my new fleecy top and my best jeans. "You're busy. Besides, it's a beautiful day. I love the cold, and I need the exercise."

"Okay, but dress warm. Can you pick up some milk and bread on the way back for me?"

"Sure. But don't expect me until about five. I've got research to do for the play." I marveled at how convincing I sounded, even to myself.

I pedaled down Old Town Road and took a right onto Elm. I continued past the library, then hung a quick left.

I felt alive and free and a little nervous. Various visions danced through my head—running into Josh or Amanda, being hit by a truck and having to explain to my parents exactly what I was doing on a back road to Keaton Corners.

I snapped out of my daydream with a nervous laugh and put my mind on the road. But I couldn't get Dylan out of my head.

"Dylan and Naomi" had a very nice sound to it. My heart felt so full, I thought it might explode. This wasn't just a stage romance. Amanda and Judi could go on thinking whatever they wanted.

I cruised down Oak Lane and into the side entrance of the Double-R parking lot. I spotted Dylan right away, just inside the open doors of the shed. He was tinkering with an old jukebox—Jonesy's jukebox, I realized. Dylan looked really great in his blue-and-white-striped coveralls.

As I approached the doors of the shed, my bike crunched across the gravel. Dylan didn't know I was coming, and I wanted to surprise him. I hopped off my bike and propped it against the side of the shop. Dylan seemed to be alone.

My heart was beating double-time as I tiptoed toward him. Strains of a folk song played on a radio in the corner as I put my hands over his eyes.

Dylan jumped and whirled around. His face zoomed from shock into megawatt joy. "Naomi, what are you doing here?" He smiled the widest smile I'd ever seen; then he looked down at his hands. They were dirty, and he quickly tucked an oily rag in his back pocket. "How did you get here?" He went over to a big porcelain sink in the corner and washed his hands. Then he looked over his shoulder at me, his face a mixture of joy and confusion.

"I rode my bike." I wanted to rush over and kiss him right away. I didn't care about my new sweater or my good jeans, but I felt a little shy. The old Naomi wasn't completely gone yet.

"I got a call this morning from some girl who wants to bring over her mother's blender. I thought you were her—"

"Do all your customers come in and put their hands over your eyes?" I joked, afraid to hear the answer.

He threw back his head and laughed heartily. He grabbed a towel and dried his hands. "No such luck! So how did you get your parents to let you come here?"

"I'm supposed to be at the library."

"Oh." His smile dimmed as he tossed aside the towel.

"But . . . I mean, Monday—"

I didn't have to say more. "Monday is so far away," he whispered. "Funny. I'd been thinking the same thing."

A second later he scooped me in his arms and spun me around, right out into the yard behind the store. We landed next to the open back door. The door leading upstairs to his room was closed, and he moved me against it. I sank back with one arm behind me and held on to the doorknob for balance.

I drank in every detail about him: the small smudge of grease on the tip of his nose, the glow in his eyes, the neatly embroidered *Dylan* on his pocket. I couldn't take my eyes off him. I was so dizzy, the ground felt up and the sky down. Then he kissed me. It was a long, wonderful kiss.

He dropped his hands from my waist and leaned back against the clapboards next to me. "I wanted to see you too," he said, not looking at me. "But I couldn't come over. I couldn't call you. I don't like this sneaking around, Naomi. Your parents, Josh . . ."

"You don't understand. This isn't easy."

"I know it's not easy." He kicked at a clump of dried brown grass.

"But maybe," I said, suddenly inspired, "maybe after the play, they'll realize you're a great actor. Not a dangerous biker. Though I did tell my dad about Mr. Cates."

Dylan looked amazed.

"He said Mr. Cates isn't dating his daughter."

We doubled over, laughing until our sides hurt.

"But I hadn't even dated you yet. I'd only kissed you." His voice dropped low. "Just once."

He reached over and ran his finger down my right cheek.

I leaned toward him. Our lips had barely

121

touched when a car drew up in front of the store.

"Bad timing!" Dylan whispered, just before he pulled away. "Must be that blender chick. This won't take long."

"It better not!" I tried to look threatening. "I'm going to keep an eye on exactly how you greet your female customers."

Dylan clutched at his heart and mocked a pained look. Then he sprinted into the shop. I hung back, still leaning against the door that led up to his place.

It was cold out, but the weak November sun shone through the bare-limbed trees. I lifted my face to the warmth and light and closed my eyes. I couldn't wipe the silly grin from my face. The more time I spent with Dylan, the more I was sure this must be love. This had to be the real thing. I didn't have to worry about any girl who came into that store. Dylan was as much in love with me as I was with him. I pinched myself. Could this really be happening to me?

"So you think you can fix this blender?" A familiar female voice floated loud and clear out the shop's back door.

My eyes popped open. It was Amanda! I gasped out loud, then clapped my hand over my mouth. What was *she* doing here?

Dumb question. She wanted to check out Dylan Russo for herself. I was sure she was here because of last night. She must have seen us at the movies.

I hung back, half tempted to peek through the

door, yet scared to death Amanda would see me now. I opted to simply eavesdrop.

"So you think you can fix it?" She sounded neutral, even sweet.

"We can fix anything." Dylan sounded proud. I was glad he didn't know who he was talking to.

Then everything suddenly got worse.

"And you came to pick something up?" Dylan sounded helpful.

"Right! My dad's snowblower." Another familiar voice, though this one was angry.

Josh! Amanda had brought Josh? This was too awful to be true. I peered around the doorjamb. I had to look, had to be sure it was him. It was Josh all right. He looked stiff and angry and very annoyed. Had he seen us at the movies too?

Somehow I doubted it. If he had seen us, he would have come over. But maybe Amanda told him later.

I ducked back before he spotted me. If I ever talked to Amanda again, she'd have a lot of explaining to do. Snooping around on her own was one thing. Bringing Josh along was another.

"The snowblower's fixed. I'll bring it around from the back. Will it fit in the trunk of your car?"

"How do you think we got it here?" Josh snapped back.

I heard Dylan's footsteps head toward the back of the shop, and I spotted the red snowblower against one wall of the shed. It looked shiny and new.

123

I ducked around the far side of the store and hid behind a tree. I didn't want even Dylan to see my face just then.

I heard sounds of lifting the heavy equipment into the trunk. Josh and Dylan talked about tying it shut. Then, a moment or two later, I heard the ignition of Josh's battered Olds kick to life. And I held my breath until I heard it pull away.

That was when I remembered my bicycle, parked in clear sight around the other side of the shop. I doubted Josh would remember what my dented black bicycle looked like or notice my blue backpack in the basket. But Amanda had come to snoop, and she prided herself on her eagle eye. She'd probably figured out I was somewhere on the premises. The thought made my stomach drop.

"Naomi?" Dylan's voice reeled me out of hiding. "Where are you?"

I came out from behind the tree and saw Dylan. And through the shop door, I could see the blender on the counter with a Fix-It tag attached.

"Is something wrong?" he asked, taking my hand.

I shook my head and pulled away. "I've got to get going." I could barely get the words out. I retrieved my bike and wheeled it around so I was facing Dylan again. "And you're right, Dylan," I said, unable to keep my voice from shaking. "I don't like this sneaking around either."

Dylan studied my face. "Good. I'm glad we agree." His eyes searched mine. I couldn't meet his glance. I couldn't tell him what had really just happened—that Josh *and* Amanda had just been in his dad's store. I couldn't tell him the truth.

"I've got to go now."

Just then a pickup truck jammed with kids pulled up to the front of the store. A couple of guys got out and headed toward us at the back of the shop.

"Yo, Dylan!" one of them shouted. "Got that generator going yet?"

"Sure thing, Riley. I'll be with you in a minute." Dylan turned to me. "I've gotta go," he said. "Tomorrow?"

"Tomorrow."

"And you'll talk to Josh?"

"Yes," I said. "I'll do that."

Once home, I realized I'd forgotten the milk and the bread.

"How will I make grilled-cheese sandwiches?" Karen grumbled, until my father promised to go out and get some.

"Didn't you drop your books off?" my mother asked as I pulled off my coat and hung it in the little closet off the back porch.

"Uh—sure." I stared at my knapsack bursting with the books. "I just brought my research home. That's all."

My mother stared at me. "You feeling all right?"

"Never better," I said, bending down to take off

my boots.

"Sometimes I think this play wasn't such a good idea, Naomi. You seem to be burning the candle at both ends."

"Oh, Mom, don't you get it? The play's the best thing happening to me these days," I declared, starting out the kitchen door.

I looked back at her and flashed what I hoped was a cheerful smile. I wasn't able to fake it. My mother had stopped washing lettuce at the sink and was now studying my face.

I actually met her glance for a moment and almost lost control. Suddenly I wanted to rush up to her, throw my arms around her, and tell her everything. Absolutely everything. The good, the bad, the scary of it all: losing Amanda, not knowing how to talk to Josh. But mostly I wanted to talk about Dylan. To say his name a hundred times. To ask her about her first love, about what it felt like. About how she felt when she met my dad. About how every inch of me felt new and open and alive. And about how I didn't want to close her or Dad or my friends out.

Talking about it with Mom would make it seem more real.

"Why do I get the feeling we need to talk?" She sat down at the counter and motioned for me to join her.

But as much as I longed to confide in her, I just couldn't at that moment. Not as long as she and my dad hated the whole idea of Dylan. I had to protect him. Maybe learning about love was something I had to do on my own.

"Not now, Mom."

She shook her head. "We've never had trouble talking before," she said, drumming her fingers against the counter. Then she got up and went back to the sink. "Ever since this play business, I'm not sure I know who you are anymore." She turned on the water.

I stared at her and felt very young and very scared, but now wasn't the time to talk. I closed my heart up again. "You know, Mom," I said softly, though she couldn't hear me over the running water. "Sometimes neither do I."

Chapter Eleven

"HI, STRANGER!" AMANDA greeted me—a little too cheerfully—at assembly first thing Monday morning.

I was sitting in the back row of the Caudwell Theater, trying to blend in with the gray upholstered seats. I had my head buried in my script, though I had known all my dialogue by heart for over a week now. I looked up and hoped I didn't look guilty. I hadn't talked to Amanda since Friday night on the phone. Though I'd sure seen her more than enough over the weekend—at the movies, at Dylan's shop. The real question was, had she seen me?

"Hi to you too." I attempted a weak smile and tried to ignore the slight note of sarcasm in her voice.

Amanda scuttled down the row of seats and sat down beside me. "Are you trying to avoid me?" she charged, plunking her book bag on the floor.

Like the plague! I replied inwardly, but I widened my eyes and tried to look innocent.

Fortunately Amanda plunged on without giving me a chance to answer. "Your hair looks pretty cool," she said, taking it in. "I can't believe you cut it without talking to me about it first! Half our lives have been spent on hair conversations." Amanda looked a little miffed.

For a heartbeat I thought my problems were over. Amanda hadn't seen me with Dylan, and she'd gotten the message to butt out when it came to Josh. "I called you twice yesterday," she added.

"You called?" I pretended to look surprised. "That's news to me."

"Your mother said you were at the library."

"I was." I dove into my knapsack for some Chap Stick.

"Funny, I didn't see you there!"

"Oh . . ." The tube of Chap Stick slipped from my hand and rolled under the seat in front of me. I scrambled down on my knees to try to reach it.

"But I did see you Saturday."

I stayed scrunched down on my knees, with my head down, for a second. Then I blew out my breath. Now I was sure Amanda knew all about Dylan and me.

I was relieved—almost. I abandoned my Chap Stick and got back up into my seat. "What were you doing at the Keaton Corners movie theater?" I asked, trying to give myself time to deal with this.

"The roller rink hadn't opened yet. Max likes *Rebel Without a Cause*. You know it's his favorite movie."

I had forgotten that. "Oh, yeah."

Amanda drew her legs up under her and faced me in her seat. "What's happening here, Naomi? What are you doing with that guy?"

I slouched down, closed my eyes, and rested my head against the back of the seat. I pressed my hands to my temples—I was suddenly getting a headache. "I'm not *doing* anything, Amanda," I said calmly. "I think I'm in love with him." There, I finally said it.

"In love!" she cried, in an extremely loud voice. Every head in the row in front of us turned around. "Mind your own business," Amanda ordered. No one, of course, obeyed.

I got up, suddenly feeling invaded. What was happening with Dylan and myself was special, private. It wasn't something to be argued about in the school theater.

"I'm outta here." I grabbed my stuff and started to move past Amanda. "I've got a headache. I'm going to the nurse." My face was burning with embarrassment, with anger. I felt like I was about to break down and cry right there—and I never cry in public.

Amanda wasn't about to let me go that easily. She ended up leading the way out into the hall and yanked me into the closest bathroom. Thankfully it was empty.

Amanda plunged right back in. "How can you be in love with someone so fast? That's impossible! And what about Josh?"

"Josh," I murmured. "Did he see me there with Dylan too?"

"Is that all you care about? Getting caught? Don't you care how Josh feels? That you've been friends forever?"

I put my hands over my ears to tune her out. I leaned back against the cool tiled wall and slid down until I was sitting on the floor. "Stop it, Amanda. I don't want to talk about this any-more."

"I do," she declared. Through the wall I could hear everyone singing "The Star-Spangled Banner." Assembly had started. If we didn't get back to the theater fast, we'd both get detention . . . unless I really did head for the nurse's office.

"Something's happened to you, Naomi."

"Yes, something has," I said, getting up off the floor. I dusted off my leggings and tugged down my sweater. "I've fallen in love."

Amanda snickered, and I had this urge to lash out at her. "It's just a fling, Naomi. He's your handsome leading man. Don't you see what's happening?"

"I see. But obviously you don't!" I snapped.

Amanda shook her head in disgust. "Love—real love—doesn't make you lie to your friends and your parents, and sneak around places, hurting people you've known forever."

I actually laughed. "Not true," I said. "Love does exactly that. Haven't you read *War and Peace, Romeo and Juliet*?"

"They're stories, just like those dumb romances you used to read. This is real life, Naomi. You're turning into a person I'm not sure I even want to know anymore."

Was this Amanda? *My* Amanda? The girl who'd been my best friend forever? "Amanda! What's happening here? You're the person I'm supposed to be able to come to, to talk about Dylan. To tell you what I feel. But you won't even listen to me about him. All you do is tell me how awful I am."

"You're not awful . . . you're just *acting* awful. And I think it's all Dylan Russo's fault. Until you met him, you were a really wonderful person." Amanda was so upset, she scared me. She wasn't just mad, I realized—she was really, truly worried.

"Naomi"—there was a hint of a plea in her voice—"don't do anything crazy. This guy . . . you hardly know him. He's swept you off your feet. You're not the sort of person to forget about everyone, everything—all for someone you know nothing about." She forced herself to look at me. "I know you spent the day with Dylan yesterday at his place."

"I wasn't up in his room, Amanda. I saw you

132

come in. I saw you spying on me. I figured you saw the bike there. You probably called my house before you went to Dylan's, didn't you?"

"Yes, I did. But I had no idea you'd be with Dylan. That you'd lie to your mother about going to the library."

"Is that why you brought Josh along on your spy mission?"

Amanda cringed. "I wasn't on a spy mission. I wanted to see what Dylan was like for myself. And Josh asked me to go along with him. His dad needed the snowblower back. Josh didn't want to risk facing Dylan alone. He's still angry about you heading off campus with Dylan for pizza and—"

"So he doesn't know about the movies?" I couldn't keep the relief out of my voice.

Amanda shook her head sadly. "No, he doesn't. And don't worry, I won't be the one to tell him. But he's going to find out sooner or later. You should really tell him before someone else does—or before he sees you and Dylan together. He's completely in the dark about what's going on, Naomi. And it's not fair. He still thinks you're going to the mall with us tomorrow night. You know we've been planning to pig out at the food court for over a week now."

I sagged back against the white tiles. They were cold and hard against my back. "Right, the mall," I repeated, feeling a little like a robot—a robot with an aching head. "I forgot about that." I hesitated, as a plan began to form in my mind. "Maybe I'll go to the mall alone with Josh. I'll talk to him then. And we'll all meet up together later, at Jonesy's."

Amanda shook her head slowly. "How can you sound so cold about it? Josh is crazy about you."

"But I'm not crazy about him, period. Let's not talk about it anymore . . . please."

"Believe me, talking to you about your love life these days is the last thing I want to do."

"This has to do with me and Dylan and me and Josh. But it has nothing to do with you, Amanda. I'm still your friend." Tears built up behind my eyes, and I tried to force them back.

Amanda pushed past me. "If I didn't think this was some temporary lovesick phase you're in, I'd swear I'd never talk to you again."

With that she stormed out the door and slammed it in my face. I threw myself against the door and began to sob. A hole had just opened in the bottom of my life and swallowed up my best friend.

When Dylan found me hours later at the boathouse, I was still sobbing.

"Where have you been? Are you okay?" he asked, bursting into the boathouse.

I was sitting on a heap of coiled rope, scrunched under a blanket and unable to control my tears. I had ducked out of the building during assembly and stumbled here, where no one would find me. I couldn't answer him through my tears.

"It's freezing!" he said, taking off his jacket and draping it around my shoulders. Then he drew me into his arms and held me. Until I felt his body heat, I hadn't realized I was cold. His hand smoothed my hair, and I held on to his sweater for dear life as I wept into his shoulders. "I've looked everywhere for you. Ever since assembly. Marnie said you weren't there, and Dana said you weren't at lunch, either. Rehearsal's in forty-five minutes. I was afraid you'd miss it."

Slowly my tears subsided. I tried to talk but could barely find my voice. I couldn't believe I had been out there for so long. A whole school day. I'd cut every class. Only a few days ago I had never cut one class in my life. I certainly was changing.

"Let's get out of here, get something warm," Dylan urged. He moved his hand beneath my coat and smoothed my back.

"I won't—I won't go back there," I stammered. I never wanted to set foot in school again.

Dylan drew me to my feet and guided me outside. I blinked at the bright light. The sky was soft and pink and silver over the river.

"Hey, what happened? Why are you crying? Did you talk to Josh? Did he give you a hard time?" A scary edge crept into Dylan's voice.

"No, it was Amanda. She saw us at the movies and she—she was the girl with the blender yesterday."

"Amanda was at the shop? The redhead?"

Dylan held me back at arm's length. "Why didn't you tell me?"

"And Josh was with her," I admitted. I rubbed my fist into my eyes and tried to wipe my face.

Dylan pulled out a red bandanna from his pocket. He gently dabbed my cheeks, then lifted my face toward his. "What's happening, Naomi? You could have told me after they left."

"I thought you'd feel bad about it." I walked farther down the path to the river. My legs were stiff and my head ached.

"I feel worse now. What's been going on with you? Are you in serious trouble because of me?" He sounded confused and hurt.

I tried to shake my head no, but I had no more strength left to lie—to anyone. "Yes, I'm in trouble." I forced myself to meet his eyes. "Oh, Dylan. I don't know where to begin." Then I sank down on a bench and told him everything—from the day the cast list was posted, to my father's reaction to the motorcycle, to my fight with Amanda that morning. "I feel like the earth just opened up and swallowed my whole life," I finally sobbed.

"Well, I'm still here," Dylan said with a catch in his voice. "If you think I'm worth it—" He broke off, taking his hand off my shoulder. I felt he was giving me space to decide.

Didn't he realize I had already decided a few days ago, after that kiss? Of course, at the time I didn't know I was choosing Dylan over everyone else I knew. But I couldn't turn back now. Amanda, Josh, even my parents—I'd deal with them somehow. But Dylan was all that mattered. He was my life.

"How can you say that!" I finally gasped.

Dylan drew me into his arms and we held each other.

But there was still one question I needed answering. "Dylan, this whole thing between us—it's for real, isn't it? I mean, I think I'm in love with you, but after this week—when the play is over and done with—"

"I'll still love you," he answered, without making me actually ask. "In fact, I wrote something for you. I was saving it until then, but—"

He got up and turned his back for a second, then came back to the bench and hunkered down in front of me. He took both my hands in his.

"I wrote you a poem," he said. For the first time since I met him, he looked a little shy. "It's not a long poem. It's small and it doesn't rhyme or anything." Then he cleared his throat, and spoke very softly into the breeze:

"When you leave,
I grow as empty as a children's zoo
In a blizzard."

"Oh, Dylan," I whispered. "It's beautiful." I couldn't say anything else. The moment was so perfect, it made my heart ache.

Overhead a faint cry made us look up. A flock of geese cut across the big pink clouds. We stood a moment watching the sky. Not touching. Not kissing.

We headed back to school for rehearsal just as the three o'clock bell rang, walking across the playing field arm in arm. I didn't care who saw us. I didn't care if I got detention. I didn't care if Josh ran into us. Nothing was going to make me hide my love for Dylan anymore.

We stopped at the student lounge to get hot chocolate, then headed for the theater.

"All this secrecy gives me bad vibes," he said as we strolled down the back hall. Most kids had already left for a football game over at Quincy High.

"So you will talk to Josh tomorrow?" Dylan asked.

"Yup, at the mall. Like I told Amanda."

"You are going to tell him, though. . . ."

I suddenly got the sense Dylan didn't quite trust me in this. "Of course. I just have to pick the right moment. We've been friends so long."

"I know. You've told me that already," he said.

I noticed Marnie coming toward us down the hall. Dylan dropped his arm from around my waist and yelled. "I found her."

"Just in time, Dylan. Judi would have your heads if you two missed this rehearsal. It's the last one before dress rehearsal Wednesday."

"Trust me. I wouldn't let Naomi let Judi down." Dylan waited until Marnie's back was turned, then reached out and drew me in for a quick kiss. "After all, what kind of Beast would I be without my Beauty?" he murmured in a soft, husky voice.

"Dylan—" I stopped him. "You weren't just looking for me because of rehearsal, were you?"

"I was looking for you because I missed you," he said simply. Then he touched my lips with his fingers as we reached the theater doors.

My heart lifted slightly. But I would have felt better if he'd said "Because I love you."

Chapter Twelve

S OME PROMISES ARE hard to keep, and I realized that the very next night at the Revere Hills mall. I had promised everyone—Amanda, Dylan, myself—that I would break up with Josh that night. But by eight fifteen I was busy dancing with him instead.

We had parked his car in front of the main entrance, and I was practicing my best breakup lines in my head. But before we'd taken five steps toward the food court, we found ourselves in the middle of a line dance. It seemed that tonight was the big Line Dance Jamboree.

A woman in a cowboy hat and a denim miniskirt stood on a small stage demonstrating the dance. Josh stared, then looked down at me and laughed. "I don't believe this. You finally conned me into going dancing."

Josh hates to dance. I love it more than anything.

"No, Josh," I protested. "I didn't con you into anything. I'm not in the mood tonight anyway."

But Josh wasn't listening. He was tapping his feet and watching the instructor teach some new line dance.

A minute later Josh had grabbed my hand and dragged me into the last row of dancers. I was glad when he let go to join in the dance. Josh had a big, friendly paw of a hand, but it wasn't Dylan's hand. I didn't want any other boy to touch me again. Only Dylan.

Dancing was good, though. It took my mind off the painful deed I had yet to do. I stopped practicing breakup lines and lost myself in the funky country beat. I don't know how long we danced, but when the band finally took a break, Josh and I moved toward the food court—our original destination—with the rest of the crowd.

I was flushed and hot, but my body felt good—loose and relaxed. We just drifted with the crowd. I had lost track of Josh for a moment, then realized I wasn't anywhere near the food court. Josh was beside me, and we were in the arcade. Little gusts of cold air shimmered through an open door that led to the alley outside—also known as Lovers' Lane.

Josh edged me through the door before I realized what was happening. He was so close to me, I could feel the heat of his body through his flannel shirt. Suddenly my back was pressed against the brick wall, and Josh was leaning against me. He began to kiss my throat, my neck, my lips in a way he never had before.

I pushed against his chest. Hard. "Josh, what are you doing!" I gasped, and couldn't stop my hand from wiping my face.

He looked a little dazed, and smiled down at me. "I think we should go dancing more often," he whispered, his voice all mushy. "I've never seen you look as beautiful as you do tonight. I feel—I feel like I'm seeing you for the first time, Naomi. I think I'm falling—"

"Josh Davidson!" I slipped under his arm and put a good two feet between us. I wrapped my arms around my chest and forced myself to look playful, to laugh, though I wanted to run away from him as fast as I could. "Now, don't go getting serious on me," I said instead. Then I looked at my watch. "Hey, we're gonna be late. We don't want to keep Amanda and Max waiting."

Then I hurried out of the arcade and let him follow me all the way back to the car. As I crossed the parking lot in the dark, I put my hand to my lips and continued to wipe away his kisses. Josh's kisses felt sinful now. As if he'd tainted everything I'd shared with Dylan.

The whole way to Jonesy's I tried to work up the courage I needed. I needed to say, "Look, Josh,

I can't see you again, except as a friend." But he kept whistling corny country music tunes and tapping his fingers on the steering wheel. Happiness poured out of every fiber of him.

I felt terrible. How was I going to do what I had to do?

Jonesy's glittered at night. Traffic crawled down South Chestnut and ganged up at the light. A large, vaguely familiar pickup truck was hogging extra spaces in Jonesy's lot.

"It's weird, Naomi, but tonight—tonight I think I'm falling in love with you."

"Oh, Josh," I groaned. But from the look on his face I could tell he thought my "Oh, Josh" was a heartfelt sigh.

We walked into the diner. Amanda and Max were at our usual table. Josh slung his arm around my shoulder and toyed with my hair. As we approached the table, Amanda looked at us, all smiles.

I knew exactly what she was thinking: Instead of breaking up, Josh and I had made up. I'd come to my senses and made the right choice. Amanda flashed me a thumbs-up. And then her expression shifted from glee, to shock, to dismay, to something I didn't understand.

I turned around and saw Dylan standing at the cashier's counter, holding a blue takeout coffee container. He was wearing his work overalls. Over his shoulder, I noticed the antique jukebox had been reinstalled. It was playing Elvis's "Hound

Dog." Dylan looked from Josh to me and back to Josh. His mouth, his beautiful mouth, curled in disgust. He just shook his head and quickly turned on his heel.

A moment later he was gone.

Josh didn't see any of this—he was too busy talking with Max. I felt the blood rush from my head and thought I would faint. I pushed away from Josh's arm and raced out of the diner.

"Dylan!" I cried into the night, looking for his motorcycle.

Then I saw the pickup. Beneath the streetlight I saw the red Double-R logo. That's why it looked so familiar. He paused at the curb, then pulled into traffic and vanished in a blur of taillights.

I stared down the crowded boulevard for a long time.

"Naomi?" Josh was behind me. Before he could touch me, I hurried down the diner steps.

"I want to go home. Now! I need to go home. Please don't look at me like that," I burst out, as Josh stared.

"Fine," Josh said, his lips drawn in a tight line. "I'll tell them we're leaving."

I watched as he stalked back inside the diner. But all I could think of was Dylan. The way he'd looked at me. How betrayed he must have felt. I sat in the passenger seat of Josh's car as we sped toward my house. I knew he was angry and confused. And I knew I wasn't being fair. But I couldn't deal with

144

it now. I had to call Dylan at the fix-it shop right away. I had to explain to him first.

Dylan loved me. Once I told him what had happened, he'd understand. He'd forgive me. He just had to forgive me.

Josh had barely stopped the car when I jumped out and raced for the porch. "Naomi?" he shouted after me.

"I'll talk to you tomorrow," I called over my shoulder. It had been the worst night of my life, but that wasn't Josh's fault.

"You're home early," my mother said from the living room. My parents were so absorbed in the TV, they didn't see the tears streaking my face.

I bolted up the front steps, grabbed the phone, and stretched the long cord into my room. I closed the door softly and sat down, my coat still on. I dialed directory assistance and got the number of the Double-R Repair and Fix-It Shop. My fingers shook as I punched them in.

"You have reached the Double-R Repair and Fix-It Shop. We are closed for the evening. If you have an emergency, dial—"

I slammed the phone down. The voice on the answering machine was gravelly and deep, not Dylan's. Probably his dad's. I decided to call Dylan at home. I'd already memorized that number.

"Yo to you. You have reached the Dylan Russo studio, otherwise known as Dylan's joint. I'm not around right now, and you know what to do at the beep."

145

I hate talking to machines, and I fought to find my voice. "Dylan, it's me. Naomi. Call me tonight. Tuesday. I don't care how late it is. Please. We've got to talk. I've got to explain. It's not—" *Bleep.* The machine cut me off. I started to dial back, but I hung up. How could I tell Dylan over his answering machine how I felt?

"I called him all night!" I wailed in the theater dressing room the next afternoon. "But he never called me back."

I sat on the floor surrounded by my long skirt and five girls I barely knew. I had never broken down in front of anyone like this, except Amanda.

I'd lost everyone who mattered to me—the guy I loved, my best friend. And I was about to lose Josh, too, because with or without Dylan, I couldn't pretend to care for him as more than a friend.

I'd never felt so alone in my whole life. Dress rehearsal for *Beauty and the Beast* would begin in five minutes, but I couldn't imagine walking out onto the stage. I'd waited all week for today—my first chance to wear Beauty's lush, romantic costume, to see Dylan's face light up when I emerged from the dressing room with my makeup perfect. As if he were my enchanted prince and I his Beauty.

Now the very thought brought a fresh round of tears.

I, who until two weeks ago was calm and shy,

was making a terrible scene. But I just couldn't help it.

Dylan had dumped me—and now my heart was broken. I wasn't sure what was worse—not having Amanda around to comfort me, or the fact that Dylan was avoiding me like the plague. That thought choked off the next round of sobs. All night long I had called Dylan. All night long I had gotten his machine.

And today Dylan had disappeared in the over-crowded halls of our school. It was the first day since we'd met that we hadn't even accidentally bumped into each other in the halls. I knew he was avoiding me on purpose. And I couldn't stand it. He wasn't even giving me a chance to explain what had happened.

How could Dylan close me out like this? How could he let me fall apart?

"What kind of person is he?" I buried my head in my arms.

Dana desperately dabbed at the rivulets of eye shadow streaking my painted cheeks. Marnie knelt beside me and handed me tissue after tissue. A few weeks ago I'd hardly known these girls, and now they had replaced Amanda. And the worst part was it was my own fault that Amanda, like Dylan, was no longer a part of my life.

Had Judi and Amanda been right all along? Did our romance only work when I was Beauty and Dylan was the Beast?

Then I thought of his face last night at Jonesy's. The disappointment, the pain, the disgust. Even Dylan Russo wasn't that good an actor. His anger had been real, all right. I knew he must be really freaked out. I sure was.

"You've got to pull yourself together. Rehearsal starts in five minutes. And you're on in eight minutes. We've got to keep to schedule today. This run-through is supposed to be exactly like opening night. *Tomorrow* night." Dana emphasized the word *tomorrow*.

Ten minutes later, as I waited in the dark wings to make my first entrance, I saw Dylan. The short prologue ended, and he swirled off stage in a cloud of rage. Dust flew up from the floorboards as he dragged his cloak behind him. On cue he turned and bellowed a Beastly yowl onto the set from the wing. The heavy mask was miked to amplify the sound. Even amplified, his yell sounded weak, hoarse, unconvincing. Then he whirled around again and slammed right into me.

His glance caught mine through the tiny eye slits in his mask. Then he continued on past me as if I were just part of the scenery.

I was stunned. "Dylan!" I cried after him. But the next thing I knew someone shoved me out of the wing and onto the stage. I stood there speechless, blinded by footlights, my head reeling. My mind was perfectly blank except for one word. *Dylan.*

I began to panic. In the dark of the audience I could see Judi's white notepad, her eyes gleaming, but nothing else. Then Dana prompted me from the sidelines. My memory kicked in, and I began to say my lines.

In the middle of my first sentence, Dylan strode right in front of me—Beast head in hand. He marched right up to the footlights and shielded his eyes.

"Judi?" he called out to the dark auditorium. His voice sounded like a gravel pit.

There was a definite pause before she answered. "What are you doing, Dylan?"

"I'm going home."

"Home?" Judi repeated in a horrified gasp.

"I'm sick. My throat. I'm pretty sure I'll be fine tomorrow, but I don't want to get anyone—uh—Naomi sick today."

My jaw dropped.

Judi cleared her throat loudly. "Okay, Dylan. It's probably just dress-rehearsal jitters, but just in case it's a cold coming on, a little rest won't hurt. You've rehearsed enough that you should be okay to go on tomorrow without today's practice. We'll just have to manage without you." She called Steve Levine, Dylan's understudy, from the back of the audience. "You don't need to change, Steve. Just wear Dylan's mask to get used to it, in case you really do need to go on tomorrow night."

Then she told Dylan to go home, drink lemon

149

tea with honey, and get some sleep. She sounded motherly, but I could tell she could see right through him.

Dylan wasn't sick and Judi knew it.

Dylan left, and the rehearsal went from bad to worse. At eight that night Judi gave us a pep talk about how dress rehearsals are always a mess, and then sent us home.

I was alone in the dressing room, putting on my shoes, when Judi walked in. She drew up a chair, turned it back to front, and sat down, straddling it.

"Hey, Beauty," she said in a teasing voice. "Want to talk about that terrible performance you just gave? Dress–rehearsal nerves are infamous, Naomi. Even without whatever has been going on between you and Dylan."

"What about me and Dylan?" I snapped with the force of a karate kick.

Judi frowned a little. "I'm not blind, Naomi."

"Well, obviously I am. Blind and stupid and a complete idiot when it comes to guys. And for your information nothing, absolutely nothing, is going on between us. Not now . . . not anymore." The forever of that hit me, and I burst into tears again. "I'm sorry," I wailed, hiding my face in my arms. "I've ruined everything. Go ahead, say I told you so. Stage romances don't work."

"They're chancy, but sometimes they do work," Judi said. I was so surprised, I looked up. "But work or not, you have to be professional about this.

That's why I'm here coaching Masques. I'm here to help you through the rough spots. Lots of crazy feelings come up even between adults when they are thrown together so much in a play. Rehearsing is a very intense sort of experience."

"You can say that again," I said, blowing my nose.

"But whatever happens, the show must go on."

All of me sagged. The show could go on, but I couldn't. No way. How could I ever face Dylan again?

"Maybe if you talked to him," Judi suggested. "Maybe you can call a truce . . . at least for the next few nights. If you get into your roles, you'll be surprised at what miracles can happen on stage. You'll forget he's Dylan Russo and fall in love with the Beast. And when the curtain comes down, you might even still hate the guy, but the next night, you can go on and make the magic happen for the audience again. Believe me. Do you think all those actors on Broadway get along, let alone like each other?"

I knew where she was coming from, but this was different. This wasn't about Broadway. This was about me and Dylan.

"Naomi." Judi touched my sleeve. "Listen to me. You're a talented actress. You've got a gift. I know it's hard to realize now, but after the next few nights, you two never even have to see each other again. You've got the rest of your life to lead, and you'll have plenty of boyfriends. But the important thing is not to throw *this* away." She waved at the

151

pans of greasepaint, the makeup brushes, the rack of costumes. "Give yourself a chance, Naomi. You know, this guy's not worth losing the joy that acting gives you."

"But he is!" I declared, jumping to my feet and grabbing my jacket. Dylan was the reason for the joy I had found the last few weeks. I couldn't even imagine acting without Dylan.

"What he *is*," Judi said emphatically, "is a very good actor, Naomi. He has a very big talent and he's going to go far. When he's on that stage, he's really into his role . . . leading man, Beast, and all."

Listening to her, my tears suddenly ran dry. "What are you saying? That he was making all that up? That everything was fake between us, and he was just acting with me? Is that it?" I felt a terrible weight on my chest and wondered if a fifteen-year-old could have a heart attack.

"No, Naomi. He's caught up in the feeling of the moment, just like you. Sometimes things, people, feelings, are not what they seem."

"I don't have to listen to this!" I shouted at her. "You don't know the first thing about me and Dylan. He's not that kind of person. He isn't. He *isn't!*" I screamed the last couple of words. I grabbed my knapsack and managed to get out of the theater before I started crying again. I bolted out of the building, into the night. A light rain was falling, and raindrops raced the tears down my face.

Chapter Thirteen

FALLING IN LOVE with Dylan was the biggest
mistake of my life. I accepted this awful truth
on my way to the bus stop that night after dress rehearsal.

At first all I could think about was how wrong
Judi was—Dylan and I were different. Ours was not
just a stage romance—this was real love. Through
my tears I could still taste Dylan's kisses, hear his
voice, see the incredible joy in his eyes when he
looked at me . . . and then the pain he must have
felt last night when he saw me with Josh.

Then everything was suddenly crystal clear.
Dylan didn't love me, not really. And he never ever
had. If he did, he wouldn't have run at the first sign
of trouble. He would have stood his ground, not
given up on me so easily. He would have believed
in me even when he saw me with Josh. He would

have swallowed his pride and called me last night. Above all, he wouldn't have abandoned me on stage tonight.

He'd faked the poem, the compliments, even those kisses. God knows, I'd fallen for the whole routine, hook, line, and sinker. He deserved an Oscar for his performance, and I deserved an award for Idiot of the Year.

Maybe Dylan really was just caught up in being a leading man. Maybe he believed his own act.

Maybe he was a truly horrible person.

I was almost at the bus shelter when Josh's voice cut across the parking lot. "Naomi?"

I turned toward it like it was a homing beacon. What I needed more than anything at the moment was a friend. An old friend.

Josh was standing by his Olds, car keys in his hand. "It's raining," he said nervously as I approached. "The debating tournament ended late, and the bus just got back to school. Need a ride home?" He stood tall and solid in the rain. "Besides, I mean, about last night. You left without saying good-bye." He stopped. "Please, Naomi. Don't do this." He opened the passenger door to his car and stood there, waiting for me to get in.

I was glad for the rain, because Josh couldn't tell I'd been crying.

"No, Josh. I don't think I want a ride home right now. But about last night . . ." With all my heart I ached to be able to look at Josh now, jump in his car, and make things between us go back to the way they were before Dylan. Fun, easy, comfortable.

But comfortable wasn't enough for me anymore. Dylan might have been faking his love, but I wasn't. In Dylan's arms I had felt as limitless as the stars, and I could never settle for anything less again. From now on it would be real love for Naomi or nothing! And I wasn't in love with Josh. I was sure of that now more than ever.

"Last night, Josh, I tried to talk to you, but you seemed so happy."

"I am happy." He smiled broadly to prove it.

"I'm not."

"I can see that." He took a step toward me and touched my hand.

I stepped out of reach. "No, Josh, don't. You know, we've been friends a very long time."

"Since sixth grade?"

"Fifth," I corrected him. Under the streetlight I saw him manage a small grin. I had to tell him the truth—get this over with fast. "I'm still your friend. But that's all I can be, Josh. I just can't date you anymore."

He shoved his hands in his pockets, threw his head back, and groaned. "It's that guy, isn't it?"

"Dylan?"

"Yeah, him. That guy in the play." Josh shook his head. "I'm such a dope. I should have seen this coming. Everything was wonderful between us until you met him. He just swept you off your feet with all that sugary romance stuff." He took a deep breath. "How can I compete with that?"

"No, Josh. That's not true."

"You're not involved with him?"

That stopped me cold for a moment. I fought for self-control. "No—yes—I don't know. Oh, Josh . . ." I started to cry again. "Dylan has nothing to do with what I'm telling you. I'm sorry, but I've *never* felt more toward you than as a friend."

Josh backed off a little. "You're much more than a friend to me," he said with great dignity. "Last night . . ." He searched for the right words. "You've been changing recently. You're more beautiful than ever, Naomi. Something about you—you're so full of—I don't know, Naomi. I know this sounds corny, but you seem so alive lately."

My heart stopped. Alive. Yes, that was how acting—and Dylan—had made me feel. I was starting to take chances. I was beginning to believe in my own dreams. I had taken the first small step with that Masques audition, and since then everything had changed in my life. Josh had fallen in love with the Naomi I'd become since Dylan, since the play, since I'd stopped hiding from my dreams.

I swallowed back my tears. "I'm sorry, Josh. I can't change how I feel for you." I felt like a jerk as I said this.

"And this guy—Dylan—"

I shook my head and shrugged. "I don't know. I

think I'm in love with him, but it . . ." And then I broke into tears again.

For all the time Josh had known me, he'd never seen me cry before. And now I couldn't stop. Josh quickly gathered me in his arms, and I sobbed into his damp denim jacket. He massaged my shoulders with his hand.

I pulled away and suddenly felt very lonely. "No, Josh. I meant what I said about us. I can only be your friend . . . if you can live with that."

Josh looked lost, but he managed a smile. "I can live with it—eventually. I'll need some time to sort things out. But . . . well, how many people can say they've been friends since the fifth grade?" He jangled his keys and pointed to his car door. "The offer of a ride still holds."

"No. It's too awkward. Besides, I think we both need to be alone."

Josh slammed the passenger door shut. He gently touched my cheek with his hand as he quietly walked by me. "Good night, Naomi."

"Good night, Josh," I said as I watched him climb into the car.

As he drove away, I heard a familiar sound from across the parking lot. But that was impossible, my mind insisted. He'd left rehearsal hours ago. I turned around, and my heart leaped up as I saw the Harley pull out of the shadows. It was dark, but I knew it was Dylan. He pulled under the streetlight and stopped. The look on his face when he saw me and Josh scared the soul right out of me.

"Dylan!" I yelled into the night. "It's not what you think. Don't leave. It's not what you think!"

Dylan's scorn hurt like a punch in the chest. "How could you possibly know what I'm thinking?" His voice was filled with thorns and needles and swords.

I stopped just short of his bike and felt like the wind had been knocked out of me. I didn't know someone could hurt me so badly.

He yanked on his driving gloves and grabbed the handlebars of his bike.

I put my hands to my face and couldn't believe my eyes. Dylan had turned up here, against all odds. And against all odds he had seen me with Josh— again.

And now he was moving away fast. He was going to leave me again. I told myself this couldn't be happening. Not now, after I'd finally managed to end things with Josh. There had to be a chance I could make everything right. I wouldn't let Dylan believe the worst of me.

I planted myself in front of the Harley and fought to find my voice. "Don't you get it? I just broke up with Josh!"

"That's a bit hard to believe." His voice was soft and controlled.

I wanted to shake him to his senses. Didn't he understand? I'd really hurt one of my best friends,

158

just so I could be with him. Casting off friends wasn't like casting off socks. Not for me. I usually made friends slowly and planned on filling my life with them forever.

Dylan—no—*love* had changed all that. I only wanted to fill my life with Dylan forever.

"You seem to make a habit of hugging and kissing guys you break up with."

"That's not fair!" I shouted. "I've never hugged or kissed any guy but you and Josh. Josh doesn't count. You know that."

"You've got a funny way of showing it." Dylan had been so sweet in love, but in hate he was bitter, like poison. "Twice in two days now." He wasn't smiling anymore. His eyes were pained. His normally loose body was tight with anger.

He'd shut me out. Closed me off. "Don't lock me out," my mother had said. Now I knew how rotten she'd felt. Dylan had slammed the door in my face and locked me out of his heart.

"You just don't know what the truth is anymore, Naomi. I trusted you. You broke your promise to me, and I don't like people who break promises. I have to trust my own eyes, and I know what I saw. I think you're a liar."

"I can't believe I'm hearing this." I wrapped my arms around my chest and tried to ignore the rain. My throat ached from crying. "I never lied to you. Never. All I did was hug Josh. I've known him all my life. I can't just throw him

159

away. Say, 'Hey, I don't love you, so get lost.' "

Dylan's eyes glittered in the light of the street-lamp. His expression was grim. How could anyone turn love off so easily?

The rain pelted my face, but I couldn't move. I couldn't stop searching his face. Only hours ago this was a boy I'd never wanted to stop touching. Now I realized I barely knew him.

The last two weeks suddenly seemed unreal as I wiped the water off my face. I couldn't stop looking at him. Waiting. Hoping he'd say, "Hey, enough of this. Let's start this whole thing over again. Give it a happy ending."

But Dylan only lifted the kickstand of his bike, turned up his jacket collar against the rain, and put his key in the ignition.

"What's going on here?" Josh yelled out of the window of his Olds as he pulled up alongside me. He hopped out of the car and planted himself between me and Dylan. In the cold, dark rain, he towered over Dylan. Sweet, gentle Josh actually looked threatening.

"What are you doing here?" I gasped, wiping the rain off my face.

"The rain got worse. I wanted to drive you home."

"Be my guest," Dylan grumbled, but he didn't turn away. He glared first at Josh, then at me.

"This guy giving you trouble?" Josh managed to sound almost burly.

160

"What's it to you?" Dylan got off his bike and kicked down the kickstand.

I couldn't believe they were actually sizing each other up. They looked on the verge of a fight. Over me. I found the whole idea horrifying. "Hey, you two, cool it!" I shouted into the wind. "I'm fine, Josh, and I meant what I said before. I'd still rather take the bus home."

Josh hesitated. Dylan stood in front of his bike. Both were getting drenched. Suddenly I didn't care about either of them anymore.

"Do what you want!" I cried. "If you feel like drowning out here, that's your business." Then I turned my back on both of them and fled through the torrent toward the deserted bus stop. As I raced across the parking lot, I heard Josh's Olds start up. Through the sheets of rain, I watched him turn down the street and head toward home.

Then the bus came, and passed the stop just as I reached the shelter. I shouted after it, letting out an angry yell.

I didn't hear Dylan pull up. "Get on!" he shouted.

"Get out of here," I called back.

He grabbed my arm. I yanked it away.

"You missed the bus. You'll be here for an hour with this storm. Get on!"

I glared at him and stared up at the bus shelter. Some kids had destroyed the roof on Halloween, and now the rain poured through the hole. Then the streetlights flickered. Once. Twice. And then all the lights, all over town, went out—like they often do in bad storms around here. The beam from Dylan's headlight was a brilliant jewel in all that darkness.

I realized I'd probably drown before the next bus turned up. I felt so powerless. But I couldn't wait here in the rain. It was getting late, and it probably wasn't safe. I grabbed the extra helmet from Dylan's hand, hopped on the back of the seat, and gripped the side handles so I wouldn't have to touch him.

The ride home was slow. Dylan coaxed his Harley around wheel-deep puddles, down pitch-black streets. Traffic had been swallowed up by the storm. At any other time I would have thought this was romantic—only Dylan and I left in the whole world, alone on a motorcycle. But I was finished with dreams of romance. If this was what love did to a person, I never wanted to fall in love again.

By the time we hit my block, I was soaked to the skin. Dylan drove right up to the front of my house. It didn't matter if anyone saw us, though I knew no one would. Dad, Mom, and Karen were at her school for Parent-Teacher night.

I stumbled off the bike, handed him the helmet, and ran through the darkness to the side porch without looking back. My hands were shaking so hard, I could barely pull the keys out of my pocket. In the dark I couldn't even see the lock on the door.

And I never heard him pull away.

Amanda, however, did.

I was on the porch, feeling for the keyhole in the door, when the beam of a flashlight bobbed toward me across the lawn.

"Naomi Peters, you're really losing it now! Tell me that wasn't a motorcycle I just heard pull down the street in this rain. Tell me that wasn't Dylan."

Amanda was always a right-to-the-point sort of person. And even though she was on the verge of deserting me for life, she was still willing to help me. She climbed up on the porch, water streaming off her yellow slicker, and aimed her flashlight at the door until I was able to get it open.

"Thank you," I said curtly as I stepped inside. I turned around in the doorway, hoping she wouldn't follow me inside.

"You're soaked," she stated. "You're also insane. You could have been killed on that motorcycle in this storm." She pushed past me and propped the flashlight on the window ledge in the mudroom. "Not that you don't deserve it. Hurting an incredible person like Josh merits some pretty bad punishment."

"Josh? You've spoken to Josh already?" I sloughed off my jacket and hung it on one of the wooden pegs inside the porch door. "I barely finished talking to him twenty minutes ago."

"You broke up with him."

"You knew I was going to do that." I kept my

back toward Amanda and stood first on one leg, then the other, taking off my boots.

"I knew. But I hoped you'd change your mind." Amanda took off her slicker and wrung out her hair. She grabbed a towel out of the laundry basket on the bench and tossed it to me. I shook out my wet hair and began to dry it. "I can't believe you just dropped him like that. And for a loser like Dylan."

"I didn't 'just drop' him, Amanda. I told him we could still be friends."

"That was big of you," Amanda said as the streetlights outside the window blazed back on. In the kitchen the refrigerator whirred to life, and the light my parents had left on in the front hall shone again.

"I can't believe you really did it. Josh is worth a thousand Dylans."

The idea was ludicrous. "Maybe to someone, Amanda, but not to me."

"I miss you, Naomi," she said suddenly.

"I was just thinking the same thing," I said as I pulled off my wet sweater and put on one of my dad's dry, oversized sweatshirts. "Tonight at the dress rehearsal I cried and cried about Dylan." Just the thought of it made me sad again. I couldn't imagine ever facing Dana or Marnie or even Judi again. Everyone knew what a fool I'd been over Dylan. "Other people were there for me, but you weren't, Amanda. The only person who ever mattered. I thought when I fell in love, I'd be able to tell you everything . . . share everything. I thought we'd be each other's best friends forever, and that there wouldn't ever be anything I couldn't tell you. But you weren't there for me, Amanda."

"How could I be there?" Her voice quavered. "I'm not involved with Masques. You've decided to hang out with a whole new crowd. I never see you anymore."

"I don't throw away friends," I told her, heading into the kitchen. Amanda followed. We sat down at the table.

"You got rid of Josh. Oh, I know you're supposed to stay friends and all, but I bet it won't happen. I'm going to miss the four of us. I wish you'd never met Dylan," Amanda said with passion.

"Ditto," I admitted quietly.

Amanda sat up straighter. "Say that again?"

"Meeting him has changed everything. Tonight I wished I could go back to the beginning and make all that's happened go away. Everything was easier before Dylan."

"I thought you were in love with this guy."

"I know I'm in love with him . . . but right now he doesn't love me."

"Then I guess I'll have to get to know him."

"Haven't you heard a word I said? We broke up tonight. He never wants to see me again. Believe me, I know that's a fact." And at the moment I wasn't sure I wanted to see him either. Then I realized what Amanda had just said. "You want to get to know him?"

"I don't want to, but I guess I'll have to if he's going to be dating you."

"But we're not dating anymore."

"Not to worry," Amanda said, reaching for the fruit bowl and peeling herself an orange. "Tomorrow night's the play. You'll see each other then."

"Not if I have anything to do about it. I've made up my mind. I fell in love with acting, but I'm going to put it all on hold for a while. After Dylan graduates in June, I'll go back to it. Judi saw what happened tonight. She'll understand."

Amanda glared at me. "I can't believe I'm hearing this. You've never quit anything. First Josh—" Amanda cut herself off. "Okay . . . forget Josh. But you have made a commitment to this play, and you're going to stick with it. Masques isn't about you and Dylan. It's about a whole group of kids who've worked really hard together to make something wonderful happen. You can't leave them now. You'll be letting everyone down. I won't let you do that." Amanda laughed and added, "Actually, *you* won't let you do that. It's not your style."

I gazed in awe at Amanda. I guess she really did know me. I'd never let anyone down in my life before, and I couldn't start now. "You're right. But Amanda, put yourself in my shoes. Imagine breaking up with Max and then having to kiss him—*pretend* to kiss him—the next day."

"You have to talk to him, Naomi. Get everything out in the open. Maybe you'll just end up working together. Hating each other's guts when the curtain drops, but giving your best to this play. Or maybe something else will happen."

"I can't do it. I can't talk to him before the play. He'll avoid me all day tomorrow. There's no way."

"Trust me, Naomi," Amanda said, reaching for her coat. She had a funny, I've-known-you-forever sort of look on her face. "When it comes to Dylan, you'll find a way."

Chapter Fourteen

AMANDA WAS RIGHT, as usual. I found a way to talk to Dylan the next day. Actually, it was really very simple.

I woke up the next morning to the sun pouring through my window—and an idea. "What's one more lie?" I whispered to myself as I climbed out of bed.

Ten minutes later I was on the local bus to Keaton Corners, though my mother thought I was meeting Dana and Marnie for an opening-night breakfast.

Fifteen minutes later I was at the intersection across from the Double-R Repair and Fix-It Shop. The door at the bottom of the stairs to Dylan's place was open, and I saw his motorcycle boots there.

He hadn't left yet.

I took a deep breath and thought I'd lose my nerve if I stood there one second longer. I grabbed the banister and climbed the steps toward his room.

It was a short flight of stairs, but by the time I reached the top, my heart was pounding. I took a deep breath and knocked on the door.

A second later Dylan opened it. He looked like he'd seen a ghost. "What are you doing here?" he demanded as he continued buttoning his shirt.

"We need to talk. Last night was all wrong. I don't know if I can make things right between us, but tonight there's a play to put on, and I can't go through with it feeling like this." I remembered something else Amanda had said. "We have to clear the air."

Dylan sucked in his breath. "Yeah. Something like that." He frowned slightly. "I'll be down in a minute." He closed the door in my face.

I fled down the steps and outside. I felt nervous.

True to his word, Dylan clattered down a few minutes later. "It's too cold to talk here. Let's get coffee on the way to school."

"Sure," I said, though I hated coffee.

He went into the shop and came out with a set of keys. He motioned me toward one of the pickup trucks. The whole time, he avoided my eyes.

I climbed in beside him. He'd put his knapsack and the gym bag he always carried to rehearsal on the seat between us. As he started the truck, I fastened my seat belt, wondering where we were headed, what kind of place he'd pick to talk. I had a strong feeling we wouldn't do much talking till we got there. Dylan's body language said, "Danger. Keep out. Hands off."

The last place I expected to end up was at Jonesy's.

Dylan led the way in and headed straight for the third booth from the door on the right. He'd led us directly to my crowd's booth.

Dylan was up to something, and I didn't like it.

We sat down across from each other, and Dylan ordered coffee. I ordered hot chocolate and kept looking out the window, over my shoulder, just to see who was coming in. No one usually had time for Jonesy's before school, but with my luck lately, Josh or Amanda or Max would probably walk in on us.

All at once I realized I didn't care anymore. In fact, let them walk in. Let them see us together. I was determined to make things work with Dylan. Amanda was ready to accept that. Max and Josh would have to too.

"So . . . are you expecting someone else?" Dylan's pointed question made me jump.

"No. Of course not," I said.

Our eyes met then, and I knew this would never work. Dylan was a closed book. My heart sank.

"About clearing the air—who goes first?" Dylan asked.

I shrugged, not quite ready to trust my voice just then. I poked my spoon into the mound of whipped cream on top of my hot chocolate.

"Then I will." Dylan ripped open three packets of sugar and dumped them into his coffee. "I was unfair to you last night. I shouldn't have called you a liar. I was freaked out, but that's no excuse. I know you're not a liar."

"I know that's supposed to make me feel better," I said. "But it doesn't."

"I'm sorry."

"So you understand about Josh?"

"I don't know about that, Naomi. Maybe he's just a friend to you, and that's okay. But I keep getting this feeling that Josh is the good guy here and I'm the bad guy. You know, the forbidden apple, all that stuff."

"You want the truth," I said quickly. "The truth is, when I met you, you were more romantic than anyone else I'd ever known. You seemed different."

"A bad boy from the wrong side of town. Maybe you just wanted to prove something to your friends." He sounded bitter, hurt, angry. He kept his eyes focused out the diner window.

"Hey, that's not how I feel. Besides, you're not that bad."

He flashed me a warning look. "Then why do you keep checking to see who's coming in? Are you afraid someone will see us together?" He was looking at me now. His eyes searched mine as if he could find some answer there.

"This has nothing to do with Amanda or Josh. It

171

has to do with us. I—I really care for you, Dylan." Love seemed the wrong word for this morning. Love suddenly seemed too big, too far away.

Dylan's brown eyes glistened as he looked up from his coffee. I watched him fight back tears. "I don't care for you at all, Naomi," he said, and what was left of my heart crumbled. "I love you," he said. "But I don't know what to do about it. I've thought a lot about us. So much has happened between us so fast, and I'm not sure where we fit into each other's lives."

"Me neither," I slowly admitted. "Dylan, I can't tell where the actor ends and you begin. I can't tell what's real anymore. I thought if you really cared for me, you wouldn't have jumped to such crazy conclusions when you saw me here with Josh Tuesday night. People who love each other don't give up so fast."

A jumble of emotions raced across Dylan's face.

"I didn't give up on you, Naomi. I avoided you yesterday because I couldn't bear to be with you. I thought if I touched you on stage during that rehearsal, I'd forget about everything bad that had happened. I'd forget to even ask you about Josh. I'd hug you and kiss you and my world would be whole again. And I'd never find out the truth."

"Oh, Dylan, I thought such awful things about you."

"But I didn't give up on you. I drove around for hours after I left rehearsal yesterday just trying to figure things out. I came back to tell you that, and I saw you hugging him again. It felt like a slap in the face. I decided I never wanted to feel that way again."

I was numb. Dylan really loved me. I should have felt happy, ecstatic.

Instead I felt doomed. Dylan loved me, and I loved him. But somehow we weren't hugging and kissing and back together again. Something was still terribly wrong.

Dylan asked for the check. "About tonight," he said, suddenly sounding all business. "The show must go on, and all. Speaking for myself, I can pull it together. I know you can too. Remember, we're not Dylan and Naomi on stage. I'm the Beast, and you're Beauty. As long as we stay in character, everything will be okay. Can you handle that?" he said.

"Handle it?" I repeated. Dylan kept looking at me until I nodded, but my heart was in my throat.

Loving each other was supposed to make everything all right. But as we left Jonesy's, everything felt absolutely wrong. We didn't hug. We didn't touch. We didn't kiss each other.

But later that day I'd have to kiss him in front of a roomful of strangers. What if his kiss was a fake one? What if I felt nothing?

What if when the curtain fell, it was the end of the story of Dylan and Naomi?

Chapter Fifteen

OPENING NIGHT FINALLY arrived. On stage Marnie's crew quickly tacked down last bits of scenery. Dave Martin strode back and forth in the Beast's rose garden, stretching his legs and softly warming up his voice. On the other side of the curtain, programs rattled and the audience buzzed.

Thirteen hours had passed since Dylan and I had "cleared the air" at Jonesy's. The play was about to begin now, and Dylan was nowhere to be seen.

I stood in the wings, covered in paisley and blue silk, while Dana touched up my wig with a curling iron.

How was I supposed to perform after experiencing the most tortured day of my life? "How can I go through with this?" I moaned.

"Forget yesterday," Dana soothed. "That was dress rehearsal. Today's the real thing. You'll see.

It'll all pop together like pieces of a puzzle. It happens every time."

I tried to listen to Dana. She was a senior, after all, and had been in Masques since her freshman year. I was inexperienced. I was nothing. But I was still in love with Dylan, and our talk that morning had left me more confused than ever. I wasn't sure if we'd made up. Neither of us had even mentioned the word *friend*. I'd rather die than be "just friends" with Dylan.

"As for Dylan," Dana whispered in my ear, "he seems more himself today. Did you guys work something out?"

I didn't trust myself to talk about Dylan then. "I don't know" was all I said. I wondered what would happen when we performed our first scene together. I couldn't imagine saying my lines to him, being near him. And I certainly couldn't picture kissing him, unless I knew we were back in love again.

"Stage places!" Andrea, the assistant director, whispered hoarsely.

Wearing his scary mask, Dylan materialized in the opposite wing. Dave took his place next to the fake rosebush. And the play began.

The stage lights flicked out and the audience fell silent. Behind me Judi cued a tape of incidental music and sound effects we were using for the play.

The curtain swooshed open. The footlights flared to life. Marnie worked her magic with the spots, and my legs began to wobble.

175

"Easy," Judi said, coming up behind me. She put her hand on my waist. "Take some deep breaths. Relax," she said, then made room in the wings.

The short prologue ended, and Dylan made his exit into my wing, swirling his cape. He turned and bellowed through his mask. I shivered. It wasn't Dylan bellowing. It was the Beast who really roared. Then he faced me. I didn't know what to expect. I prayed he wouldn't walk out on the play . . . leave me stranded in the wings again.

"Break a leg, Beauty," he murmured as he slipped by me. "Remember, I'm the Beast."

Then someone shoved me on stage, and the curtain went up for act one. The footlights glared, the heat from the spotlight above my head made me woozy. For a second I looked past the footlights and saw the faces in the audience. My stomach lurched, my hands shook, I forgot my lines.

"Father, you're back at last . . . and safe," Marnie prompted.

"Father, you're back at last . . . and safe." I started toward Dave.

"Beauty"—he hugged me to him hard—"I never thought I'd see you again." Tears filled his eyes, and I became Beauty . . . not Naomi.

By the time the second act opened, Dylan had become the Beast for me. I recoiled in horror as he welcomed me to his castle. We played scene after scene, and slowly I fell in love with this poor, solitary creature.

Yet all along I knew I was acting. I began to match the Beast's pacing, to time my lines. Behind his mask his eyes glowed with pleasure.

I felt the audience catch its breath the first time we danced across the stage.

I felt powerful. I had made the audience react. Together with Dylan. Beauty and the Beast. Our fairy tale had come to life.

And then it was time to rush from the wings for the last scene, to hurry through the Beast's garden. Desperate to find him, I raced up the small steps onto the tiny platform that filled half the stage, then down the steps again, giving the impression of running a great distance.

The Beast was lying beneath his rosebush, a battered, moth-eaten creature. He was curled in on himself, and it seemed as if he really wasn't breathing. "Oh, Beast," I cried from the bottom of my heart. "Don't die!"

He was no longer the Beast, but my prince. He turned slowly, and the audience gasped. This was certainly the most handsome prince Revere High had ever seen.

Then he wrapped his arms around me and turned his back to the audience, just like we'd practiced. Before we came together for our kiss, our eyes met. "Beauty," he whispered in a voice that carried to the back of the theater.

177

"Naomi," he murmured so only I could hear him, as our lips finally met.

Dylan, my heart sang. My soul soared and my knees went weak, but Dylan was strong and held me steady. Then he picked me up and spun me around. It wasn't in the script, but I didn't care. The play was over. We weren't acting anymore.

We were still kissing when the curtain fell. The applause was thunderous. We hadn't stopped kissing when the curtain rose again. And I barely noticed. I only knew my dream had come true. I was back with Dylan, and nothing would stop us from loving each other again.

Suddenly everyone was clapping, on stage and off. "Hey guys, the play is over. Break it up!" Judi yelled, laughing.

We sprung apart. I turned as scarlet as the Beast's rosebush, and Dylan flushed a deep pink. He gingerly took my hand. I took Dave's hand and the whole cast came forward for bows.

I think there were three curtain calls. Dylan said four. Judi said we deserved about a million more. When the clapping finally stopped, we all stayed on stage behind the curtain, laughing and yelling and screaming and crying all at once. People were pounding my back.

Families and friends made their way backstage. And in all the commotion, Dylan never once let go of my hand.

"Oh, Naomi, we're so proud of you," Mom said. "And that Dylan, what an actor. Maybe he's not as bad as we thought." She whispered that last part in my ear.

"Well, looks like we've got ourselves a real actress in the family," Dad added. "Great performance, honey. And, Dylan, you were quite the Beast."

"Thanks, Mr. Peters," Dylan said.

Somewhere in the middle of my parents' congratulating us, Amanda, Max, and Josh appeared.

"You were fantastic!" Amanda shrieked. "I'm so happy for you, Naomi. You too, Dylan."

"Yeah, you both really blew that audience away!" Max chimed in.

Then I looked up at Josh. He grinned foolishly at me but just glared at Dylan. Dylan glared back at him.

"You were great, Naomi," Josh admitted. He awkwardly moved his hand forward, as if to shake mine, so I stood on tiptoe and pecked his cheek instead. Some girls hanging around backstage gawked at him.

"Thanks, Josh. And thanks for coming," I told him. I really meant it.

"You were okay too," Josh muttered to Dylan. You could cut his reluctance with a knife, but at least he'd said it. If nothing else, Josh had guts.

Dylan nodded and looked a little embarrassed.

"Uh—thanks, man." He offered his hand, but Josh ignored it.

The tension was broken when another round of well-wishers arrived. Dylan took advantage of the commotion and whisked me off behind the backdrop. He gathered me in his arms right there in the middle of the ropes and ladders and wires.

"You were incredible tonight," he said, a little breathless. He fingered my fake curls and made a face. He carefully lifted the wig off my head and tousled my hair. "No matter what else happens to you, don't give this up. You're a born actress," he said, and his eyes shone like stars.

"You too." I wanted to hold him close and never let him go. "An actor, that is. You make a pretty good prince."

"Don't let the outfit fool you. I'm just your basic guy in coveralls," he reminded me.

"I'll keep that in mind," I murmured, beginning to feel a little dizzy.

"About tonight," he began. He looked a little dazed, as if he were having trouble keeping track of his thoughts. I know I was. "I told you what would happen if I let myself near you. I'd forget everything and never want to let you go."

"Me too." But there was still one last thing I needed to know. "I was afraid the end of *Beauty and the Beast* would be the end of Naomi and Dylan."

"Oh, no, Naomi," he said with great feeling. "It's only just the beginning."

Tears blurred my eyes as he gathered me to him. I touched his earring and whispered softly, "I love you."

"I love you, too." He smiled, then sealed my lips with a long, sweet kiss. My fairy-tale romance had finally come true.

Do you ever wonder about falling in love? About members of the opposite sex? Do you need a little friendly advice and have no one to turn to? Well, that's where we come in . . . Jenny and Jake. Send us those questions you're dying to ask, and we'll give you the straight scoop on life and love in the nineties.

DEAR JAKE

Q: *I really like this guy Robert and I think he likes me too. He's asked me out a few times, but it always ends up being a group date—me, Robert, and ten or more of his closest friends. I have fun with them all, but I'd like to date Robert . . . alone! What can I do to let him know I need some one-on-one time together—you know, just the two of us?*

J.H. New York, NY

A: This is an easy one. Simply tell Robert how you feel. Let him know you enjoy spending time with all his friends, but sometimes you need a little quality time alone with him. If Robert doesn't agree, then it may be time to reevaluate your relationship. He may be afraid to be alone with you—even the coolest guys sometimes get nervous in solo situations. And if this is the case, you need to comfort him with the knowledge that you won't bite . . . unless he wants you to. Communication is key to any relationship and this is a perfect example where a problem may be easily resolved with a little chat.

Q: *I'm a freshman in high school and I love acting in plays at my local community theater. There's this guy in the cast who's older than I am—he's already graduated from my high school! He's a total hunk and really nice, but he's so much older. The other day he asked if I'd like to go out with him sometime. I'm dying to go, to get to know him better, but the age difference is really bothering me. I'm afraid he'll pressure me to do things I'm just not ready to do. Am I being silly or do all older guys expect a date to end in bed?*

L.M. Houston, TX

A: I can't answer for all older guys out there, but there are some gentlemen left in the world—I don't think I'm the only one. Be sure this guy knows how old you are before you agree to the date. And find out how your parents feel. If it's okay with them, tell him you'll go, but pick a public activity. Go to a movie, out to dinner, ice skating, or even bowling. Don't put yourself into a situation that has the potential to make you uncomfortable. After your first date, you should have a better idea about him. Then it's completely up to you to continue seeing him or not, and to move forward as fast . . . or as slowly as you want to.

DEAR JENNY

Q: *My best friend, Megan, has been dating Dan for two years. She went on a family vacation a few weeks ago, and Dan and I hung out together while she was away. One night, while watching a romantic movie on TV, we got carried away . . . and* *we kissed! It was only one kiss and it really didn't mean anything to either one of us. It was a once in a lifetime mistake, and we both feel* awful *about it. Dan's still in love with Megan, and neither one of us wants to hurt her. We just can't decide if we should tell her about it or if we should keep this our little secret. Help!*

D.B. Huntington Beach, CA

A: Secrets, no matter how small, always seem to escape. And smaller things have been known to ruin friendships. Guilt is often the result of a secret such as yours, and both you and Dan seem to be feeling it pretty strongly. Eventually you'll begin avoiding Megan and Dan. And she'll begin to suspect you're keeping something from her. Or worse, she'll find out about your kiss from someone else. Maybe Dan will confide in a friend, who'll tell two friends . . . and so on, and so on, and so on . . . until the secret slowly gets back to Megan. I think for once Mom was right—honesty is the best policy. Tell Megan about the kiss—that it only happened once—and how bad you feel. Megan will probably be upset, but if she's a good friend, and she certainly seems an important part of your life, hopefully she'll learn to forgive you—and Dan—in time.

Q: *There's a big dance coming up at school and I really want to go. All I need to do is find a date. So far one guy has asked me to go with him, but I'm totally not interested. Normally I'd just say, "No thanks," but I'm afraid that no one else will ask me. And*

I'd rather die than go to the dance without a date! I'm also worried that as soon as I say yes to this guy, somebody better will ask me and I'll have to turn him down. What would you do, Jenny?

H.B. North Platte, NE

A: First of all, you can't string this guy along while waiting for someone better. Talk about selfish! Think about this guy for a moment. If you wait till the last minute to make up your mind, when you finally break the news that you're going with someone else he won't have time to make other plans. You need to make up your mind *today* and give this guy an answer. Is the dance really worth spending an evening with someone you don't even like? And once you've told him no, don't be surprised if other guys start asking you to go. The grapevine knows everything—who's asking who and if anyone is free. And now you'll have the freedom to accept any other offers. Also, there's nothing wrong with going to the dance with a group of friends. You'll have a better time this way—assuming the guy of your dreams hasn't appeared at your door.

Do you have questions about love? Write to:

Jenny Burgess or Jake Korman
c/o Daniel Weiss Associates
33 West 17th Street
New York, NY 10011